LAWLESS RANGE

From the moment Jim Reed, a stranger in
town, drove the Concord stage into the
wild, wide-open town of Outpost, he was in
constant danger. For in the stage were
two dead men—the driver and Johnny
Drennan, a cowhand who worked for Brad
Gulistan, one of Outpost's largest ranchers.
Accused of murder by aroused towns-
people, especially by Johhny's sister, Sally
Drennan, Jim Reed proved his innocence
by producing a consignment of gold which
he had safely brought to Outpost. At the
same time Reed identified Johnny Drennan
as one of the band of outlaws which
had shot up the stage. Immediately Brad
Gulistand was accused of secretly leading the
outlaws terrorizing Outpost with rustlings
and killings.

Books by Charles N. Heckelmann
in the Linford Western Library:

FIGHTING RAMROD
HARD MAN WITH A GUN
TWO-BIT RANCHER
LET THE GUNS ROAR!
THE RAWHIDER
LAWLESS RANGE

CHARLES N. HECKELMANN

LAWLESS RANGE

Complete and Unabridged

LINFORD
Leicester

First Linford Edition
published March 1989

Copyright © 1945 by Arcadia House, Inc.
Copyright renewed 1973 by
Charles N. Heckelmann

British Library CIP Data

Heckelmann, Charles N. (Charles Newman), *1915–*
Lawless range.—Large print ed.—
Linford western library
I. Title
813′.54[F]

ISBN 0-7089-6677-2

Published by
F. A. Thorpe (Publishing) Ltd.
Anstey, Leicestershire
Set by Rowland Phototypesetting Ltd.
Bury St. Edmunds, Suffolk
Printed and bound in Great Britain by
T. J. Press (Padstow) Ltd., Padstow, Cornwall

For A.H.

1

DUST boiled up in a swirling gray fog around the high-wheeled Concord stagecoach as it rumbled down a long, narrow grade past clumps of mesquite and prickly pear. In the west the dying afternoon sun teetered precariously above a ragged line of peaks and buttes, its scarlet rays slanting angularly along the Concord's weatherbeaten panels, before it dropped out of sight behind the hills.

But the glow in the sky remained like a giant, blood-red hand upon the drifting cloud wracks, while purple shadows of dusk crawled down the timbered slopes of the mountains.

Leather reins gripped firmly in big, muscular hands, Jim Reed studied the details of this unfamiliar land with a strict and unrelenting attention. He saw that blood-red hand in the west, felt the cool thrust of the night wind and a premonition of evil rippled the flesh between his shoulder blades.

Reed was a thoroughly big man, his bronzed face rugged and irregular with high cheekbones

1

terminating in a strong, square jaw. His eyes were the color of gray slate and his lips made a thin, stern slash across his skin. Wide in the shoulders, lean in the hips, his body had been cast in a hard, lithe mold by years spent in the saddle.

A hollow drum-roll of sound echoed from the loose planks of Indian Creek bridge as the Concord boomed across and traversed the silver-gray ribbon of dust that was Outpost's main street.

The blacks, scenting the end of their run and a warm feed, leaned into the traces. Their pounding hoofs beat a rhythmic tattoo on the ground, and the vibrations of that drum-roll of sound sent echoes chasing back and forth between the double row of false-fronted frame shacks that lined the street.

Interest put a bright, sharp glitter in Reed's eyes when he saw the tension that held this town in an iron grip. Townsmen stopped their aimless pacing along the walks and turned to regard Reed with a hostile scrutiny. Nearer at hand, two groups of slender, sun-bronzed men stood facing each other across the street's dust, thoroughly vigilant and watchful.

Then the batwing doors of the Stockmen's

2

Saloon swung open to spill three more men out upon the walks, and a window in the hotel was raised and a woman's head was thrust out, her eyes following the progress of the stagecoach.

Reed kicked on the brake, felt the wheels lock and halted the swaying Concord in front of the stage office. A crowd gathered swiftly, and down the street the two groups of men Reed had seen stationed on opposite walks, broke their ranks to march toward him.

Vaulting from the driver's perch, he paused to bat the dry, powdery dust from his black trousers, and let his glance rest upon a dark-eyed, lantern-jawed man who emerged from the office.

"Where's Carter and Judson?" the lantern-jawed man demanded, swift suspicion flaring in his olive-skinned face.

"If you're speaking of the driver and shotgun guard," murmured Jim Reed, "the driver's inside packin' more lead in his insides than is good for any man. The guard is dead somewhere five miles back along the stage road."

Deliberately Reed stepped to the stage and flung open the door. Val Ormand, the stage owner, thrust his head inside, then drew back. A rigid distaste etched hollow planes in his face.

"It's Hank Carter, all right," he said huskily.

"Get Doc Bushell!" somebody yelled.

"Carter's got company in there," Reed told them all.

Lance Koenig, the mild-mannered, fifty-year-old proprietor of the Mercantile, came up and had his look. Afterward, he turned and his eyes sought the two groups of men pushing their way through the fringes of the crowd, and Reed saw fear shadow the storekeeper's eyes.

"Johnny Drennan's inside," Koenig informed the crowd. "If I ever saw a dead man, Johnny is it."

Reed laid his firm hand upon Koenig's arm, swung the man back to the Concord. Together, then, they lifted out the limp body of Hank Carter, set it upon the plank sidewalk. The stage driver was a grizzled veteran of the trails. His skin was wrinkled and burned to the color of saddle leather. An ugly stain darkened his checkered shirt.

A short-legged man with ruddy cheeks, a flat nose and two chins pushed through the curious ring of onlookers. Reaching Carter, he set his little black instrument bag in the dust. He took one look at the injured driver and a dismal fatalism pulled at his lips.

4

"Can't do much for him here," Doc Bushell growled. "Carry him to my office."

"Not you, my friend," said Val Ormand, his voice brittle and challenging as he glanced at Reed. "Others can do that. You've got some talkin' to do and we'll be listenin'."

Reed shrugged and stepped aside. Three townsmen moved in and carried Carter away.

"Not much to tell," Reed said at last. His speech was calm and his sharp glance catalogued the faces in this throng with an extreme care. "A bunch of masked riders raided the stage five miles west of town. They shot Carter and Judson. Judson fell from the stage, dead when he hit the ground. There was just two of us inside—me and this gent."

Reed broke off and gestured to the lifeless figure of a young, slenderly built man being lowered to the walk from the Concord. There was wildness in the man's immature cheeks, a slack, downward curve to the mouth that hinted at weakness. Life had burned like a bright, wicked flame in his youth. But now his features were gray and placid in death. The memory of how that grim change had been wrought in one brief, violent segment of time deepened the bleak cast to Reed's features.

5

"I started to buy chips in the game when Drennan shoved a gun in my back," Reed resumed tonelessly. "He was workin' with the outlaws, I reckon, and he was primed for shootin'. It was him or me, and in the fight for his gun he got in the way of a bullet."

"It's a smooth story—"

"Jim Reed's the name," said Reed when Ormand paused.

"I think you're lyin'," Ormand stated bluntly. "That stage was carryin' a shipment of newly minted currency. It'd be a valuable haul for anyone. You guessed wrong when you said Johnny Drennan pulled a gun on you. He's a puncher for Brad Gulistan. Maybe you were—"

Reed hit Ormand then, with the flat of his palm. The blow made a ringing sound in the taut silence. Ormand staggered backward, was brought upright against the men standing behind him.

"Don't ever call me a liar," Reed warned. At this moment there was a rough, untamed look about him, and he showed a cool contempt for the mass hostility which washed so solidly against him.

Watching intently he saw how rashness laid its insidious torment upon the stage owner, saw

6

how his right hand made a claw above his holstered gun and his shoulders began to stir. Yet, something in the unsmiling hardness of Reed's face, and in the way his long arms with the unusually wide wrists hung limp and ready at his side, stayed Ormand's hand.

Not a person in this town but saw in Jim Reed a man for whom life was a succession of dark and dangerous risks, a man to whom trouble had never been a stranger and never would be. He carried one long-barrelled Colt in an oiled, thonged-down holster along his right thigh, and that gun had the look of being well used.

"I'd like to see that tooler make the grade," Reed murmured after a long interval. "If it hadn't been for him I wouldn't be here and your shipment of currency would be gone, Ormand. Carter whipped up the team and sent the animals plunging right into the outlaws. Somehow he held on to the reins until I could crawl out on the roof to take over.

"By that time we were past the renegades and they had to follow in the face of my gunfire. They gave up once we struck a narrow canyon. There was no time to pick up the shotgun guard. I made only one halt and that was to

7

make Carter a little more comfortable inside the stage."

"You sure tell it scarey," said Ormand with a sneer.

Fear still lurked in his eyes, but he was trying to bluff it out. He started to say something more, then changed his mind. And immediately Reed noticed that Ormand's attention had abandoned him, was centered upon a break in the crowd where a gray-eyed man of medium height with thinning gray-black hair stood carefully listening.

Everything about this man showed that he was a cattle rancher—his overbearing manner, his well-tailored range clothes, his thick, rope-calloused hands that told of many hours spent chasing wild-eyed steers out of the brakes and canyons, of other hours roping and branding. Behind him five grim-eyed cowhands had taken up a flanking position.

They were rough, range-hardened men and every one wore a shell belt and a holster that sagged under the weight of a loaded gun. Their manner was taut and expectant. Their eyes were never still, jumping from Reed to the sprawled body of Drennan and on among the crowd.

"It sure is mighty interesting to learn that

Johnny Drennan was in on that attempted hold-up," the rancher stated evenly. His voice lifted to a sharper note. "Isn't it, Gulistan?"

A queer, straining intensity shimmered through the punchers at the rancher's back. Then Reed saw how the mob had split on his left, how a wide, free space had been opened for another knot of men. At once, he knew he was seeing the two groups that had first commanded his attention when he'd driven the stagecoach into Outpost.

There was a strong feeling of antagonism here. A clash of powerful wills, an undercurrent of violence that whirled between two rival cattle monarchs. The crowd felt that hidden menace and looked to the big man who led the second group.

Massiveness characterized Brad Gulistan. In a land where big men were commonplace, Gulistan was huge and dominant. He was tremendously wide and heavy in the shoulders. His cheeks were broad, the eyes steel-blue with an odd, fathomless glitter in their depths.

"Meanin' just what, Wright?" Gulistan demanded truculently.

"It's as plain as the nose on your face," retorted Harry Wright. A humorless smile twisted his lips when he saw how Gulistan bridled at the reference to his bulky nose. "For the last five months outlaws have been ridin' roughshod over the range, lootin' stages and rustlin' beef. Up to now we haven't been able to find out who was behind those raids."

"And now?" prompted Gulistan, his heavy shoulder muscles pressing against the tight span of his shirt. He had set himself on widely planted boots, his head tilted forward, his lips flattened against solid, yellow teeth. He had the look of a man hungry for fight.

"And now we're gettin' somewhere," snapped Wright. He met Gulistan's surly glance squarely. "Findin' Johnny Drennan just about lays the trouble at your door. Drennan is one of your hands and if he had a part in that stage hold-up he must have been workin' under your orders. There are rumors that Jack Braley's gang is back in this section of the country. Maybe you and Braley are teamin' up to profit off our stolen beef herds."

There was an audible gasp from the mob. Men began pacing backward, anxious to get out of the line of possible gunfire. The promise of evil, cold and ominous, rolled in on the night wind.

Sudden brutality warped Brad Gulistan's countenance. He drew a ragged breath. Brittle violence crawled into his talk.

"Wright, I knew a man once who bought six feet of space in boothill for runnin' off at the mouth like you're doin'."

Behind Gulistan his crew spread out in a threatening, fan-shaped wedged. They were a grim lot, without sentiment and without fear, and now a fierce eagerness placed a shine on their tanned cheeks.

"Just say the word, Brad," murmured one puncher. His hand dropped silently and significantly to his Colt.

A feeling of doubt and uncertainty held Harry Wright momentarily still. Then a taunting voice spoke from the shadows of an alley nearby.

"Don't let him bluff you, Wright!"

Gulistan's square head with the leonine mane of dark hair lifted, and his eyes leaped beyond the throng, trying to ferret out the concealing shadows.

"You've got your nerve tryin' to make me out as a renegade," he said heavily. A wrong word or move now could start a bloody carnage that would take a toll of innocent lives. "Sure,

11

Drennan was on my payroll. Two days ago I sent him up to a line cabin to ride herd on a bunch of prime beef critters grazin' my north pasture. I haven't seen him until now. The man that says he was owlhootin' is a liar."

Gulistan broke off and his voice dropped to a lower, deadlier note. Temper kept hammering at his muscles, clouding his brain.

"I'm not through with you, Wright," he resumed. "This is not the time or place to start a range war, but I warn you that I take your kind of talk from no man." Abruptly he swung on the crowd. "How do we know this stranger is tellin' the truth about what happened. Sure, Johnny Drennan always had a wild streak but he was no renegade."

"What do you figure he was doin' in the stage, then?" Reed asked bluntly.

Gulistan gave Reed a dark, malevolent glance.

"That's none of your business," he growled.

"I thought you'd be afraid to talk," said Wright.

Gulistan's patience grew thinner and thinner.

"I'll talk, damn you, Wright," he exploded, "but so help me if you throw any more accusations against me or Drennan we'll have our battle right here and now. I don't know how Drennan got in the stage, but I can guess. He got paid the night before last. Instead of goin' up to the line cabin according to my orders, he probably rode over to Estreva for a spree.

"It's the wildness in him no one can control. I figure he gambled and drank up his wages and lost his horse in the bargain. To get back to Outpost he probably talked old Hank Carter into givin' him a free ride from Estreva."

Noticing the disbelieving look in Wright's eyes, the ripple of doubt that seemed to simmer through the crowd, Gulistan squared his broad shoulders and plunged on in greater rage.

"I know what you're all thinkin', but it ain't true. Johnny Drennan was as straight as his old man was crooked."

2

WRIGHT was watching this scene with a cheerless intensity. He and his crew remained wary and skeptical. There was no trust in this town. Each man was suspicious of his neighbor, wondering how much that neighbor knew about the damaging cattle raids, the organized outlawry. Daily that suspicion grew until it became a poison eating away at their restraint and destroying their faith.

Now Gulistan swung around and strode toward Jim Reed.

"Friend, I'd like to see the man who can outride a bunch of fast horsemen with a tired span of animals pulling a heavy Concord. Maybe there was a raid but you're not tellin' it straight—particularly about how Johnny Drennan died. There's an evil smell in the air and you're it. Right now you're going to tell me and everybody else what your game is or—"

Gulistan didn't finish, leaving his heavy talk hanging over Reed's head like the deadly

14

threatening blade of a guillotine. But there was no cringe in Reed and his craggy, bronzed features remained impassive.

"Or what?" he demanded.

"Start talkin' about yourself—what brought you here and who sent you or get out of town. We're not partial to strangers, particularly gunmen."

"Now that you put it that way, I think I'll stay." Reed spoke slowly and with deliberate insolence. "But I'll talk when I'm damn good and ready—and it will never be to you."

Gulistan drew himself to his full six-feet-three and the hate in his eyes was a grim and terrible thing to see. He hooked his thumbs in his gunbelt and braced himself squarely against Reed.

"Reed, you've got just three seconds to turn around, walk down to the livery, hire a horse and ride out of town. One."

Behind Gulistan his crew members spread out a little more and there was a fierce, bright eagerness showing on their cheeks. At this same moment all mercy washed out of Reed. Danger was an acid taste in his mouth, but now he relished that taste with savage pleasure.

"I've got a better idea," he said tersely.

15

"First, I think you're the one who is lyin' about Drennan. Second, you raise a big wind whenever you walk in Outpost so you figure you can blow any man down. But I don't bluff so *I'm* goin' to do the counting, and when I reach three you'll be the one to do the turning and the walking."

For a split second red rage somersaulted into Gulistan's features, holding his huge frame rigid and immobile. Then he grunted and came lunging at Reed.

Reed said, "One—two," and stepped in hard and fast with two swift blows. They were short and deadly. A solid left to Gulistan's belly doubled him up, tipped him forward so that his jaw made a clear target for the jolting right that exploded there and sent him reeling.

Off-balance, he fought to stay on his feet. But he tipped over the man to his left and all three went down in a threshing tangle of arms and legs. Gulistan rolled over, bellowing like an enraged bull. He came to his feet, his right hand blurring to his hip in a motion almost too rapid for the eye to follow.

The muzzle of his gun ripped free of holster leather, then he paused and his taut fingers

16

grew somewhat slack. His gun muzzle halted its upward arc.

Not three feet away, a reckless look on his saturnine face, stood Jim Reed. There was a Colt in his fist and the knuckles of his hand were round and hard and white. He uttered no warning, gave no command, yet he held Gulistan and all of his men entirely still.

Fury was gouging them with cruel spurs; their eyes were greedy for him and their hands were like hungry claws suspended above their guns. But they made no move, for at this moment they recognized that Reed was as dangerous as any man could be. The violent tumult that showed in his cheeks got to them and ruffled their confidence.

"Gulistan," said Reed slowly, his bleak gaze falling like a monstrous weight upon the cattleman, "you heard me tell Ormand that I don't like to be called a liar. It is something you should remember. Also, don't ever try to draw on me unless you're prepared to go all the way in gunsmoke."

Men were shifting their feet nervously in the dust. At any moment the bore of a gun might be thrust in Reed's back. He couldn't gauge the temper of this town, for he was a stranger here,

17

under suspicion, and tramping on unsteady ground. But there was a streak of iron in him that would not permit him to back down.

Gulistan removed his gun and gestured irritably to his crew to make no break of action. Violence still moved the rancher and his pride had been brutally stung.

"You step high and wide for a stranger in a strange town," he declared. "How long do you think you'll last?"

"I'm still countin', Gulistan."

"You're pretty tough, Reed, but you're only a man and lead in your belly won't do you any more good than the next man."

"Just be sure it isn't in the back," snapped Reed. "Three!"

Gulistan cursed as the gun in Reed's hand weaved back and forth in front of him and Reed moved a step nearer.

"All right. Come on," Gulistan growled to his crew.

They turned and started to move off, but a scuffling sound at the edge of the crowd halted them. A blocky, wide-shouldered man with an unruly mop of gray hair on his small head, pushed his way up to Reed. Behind him fluttered Doc Bushell.

"Break it up," ordered the blocky man. A yellow-gray handlebar mustache covered his thin, upper lip. At forty-eight Sheriff Ben Collier was as seamed and as weather-beaten as the calfskin vest that covered his flannel shirt. "I just rode in from Estreva. Looks like you gents have been on the prod." Collier glanced coolly at Reed. "Bushell told me your story, Reed. Carter just died. But before he went out he managed to talk. That raid happened like you said."

"Hell, I knew it!" blurted Harry Wright. He wheeled to face Brad Gulistan. "What have you to say to that? How about Drennan now?"

Gulistan was momentarily uneasy. A shadow of concern veiled his eyes.

"If Drennan was in on it," he said, fighting to keep his voice spare and even, "then he's better off dead. He was actin' on his own hook."

The slender figure of a girl brushed Reed aside.

"Get out of my way!" she cried. Then a sob tore at her throat and she added brokenly, "Johnny—you can't be—you mustn't be—"

She knelt down beside Drennan's prone shape. Her firm, round arms gathered his head

19

and shoulders against her. She shuddered when she felt the limp lifelessness of that body. After a moment she gently lowered Drennan to the ground and looked up at Collier.

"Your brother's past help," he murmured softly. Collier was suddenly old and tired. There was a look of gray resignation on his seamed face.

"Who killed him?" she asked tonelessly.

Collier nodded toward Reed. The girl swung that way. Her arms were rigid at her side. She came forward like a person in a trance.

Reed watched her with a hint of uneasiness he couldn't explain. She was a small, straight-shouldered girl. Blonde, curly hair framed her tanned oval face. Her lips made a warm and red and tremulous line against her smooth skin. She was dressed in a man's white shirt open at the throat and scuffed riding breeches and boots. There was a lonely quality about this girl— something harassed and forlorn. It showed in her blue eyes. Yet, there was strength and courage in her, too.

"You murderer!" she said, scorn chilling her tone. "Are you proud of putting another notch in your gun?"

The girl's right hand stabbed down toward

her hip. But there was no gun in the holster and she scowled.

"There are no notches, Ma'am," Reed said quietly. "Killing is never a pleasant thing."

"You should know," she answered heatedly. Her eyes raked him boldly and centered longest on his wide, capable hands, the oiled holster, the gun still sagging in his fist. "If I were a man I'd kill you and have my revenge." The fiery, aroused spirit of this girl came out of her in each gusty word. "They're saying Johnny was working with a gang that tried to hold up the stage—that he was the inside man. That is not true. Johnny has always been on the level."

"I'm afraid you're mistaken, Sally," interposed the sheriff. While the girl was speaking to Reed, Collier had been going through Drennan's pockets. Now he rose and handed Sally a fold of black cloth, each end joined by a slender loop of string, and a creased square of paper. "Here's a mask I found on him. There's a note, too, tellin' him to be on the eastbound stage out of Estreva on Wednesday. That's today. It says his job is to take care of any passengers inside."

A stricken look came into the girl's face.

The blood slowly seeped out of her cheeks, whitening the coat of smooth tan.

"These things—" she murmured brokenly. "They could have been planted on Johnny."

"But I don't think they were," insisted Collier.

Harry Wright pushed forward now, a sneering contempt twisting his acid-flowing speech.

"Blood will tell, I reckon," he said. "Old Sam Drennan was an owlhooter and died by a hangrope. Young Johnny would have lived to stretch hemp, too, if he hadn't been killed."

"Shut up!"

Temper flung that curt warning out of Reed's throat. Shaken by the virulence of his tone, Wright took an uncertain backward step, then slowly savagery returned to his face.

A voice out of the crowd suddenly took up where the rancher had left off.

"You can say what you want, stranger, but there's wild blood in the Drennans and the girl's got the same streak." The speaker's windy, irritating voice knifed into the air, subtle and goading. "We all saw her go for a gun that wasn't there. And that's the girl we've got teachin' our children in school."

"Friend, I've heard enough," murmured Reed and shouldered roughly through the crowd.

There was the sound of a hurried retreat as Reed slammed men aside and reached the alley from which the voice had issued. Reed found it empty. Dimly he heard a faint slur of steps at the far end, then total silence. Angrily he returned to the girl and the sheriff.

"I don't need your help—now," she told him.

Her eyes were cold as they touched him briefly. She was fighting against the black tide of grief. She wanted to cry but there was a fierce pride in her. So she held back the tears and her chin lifted and bitterness came into her voice.

"None of you ever gave Johnny a chance," she flung at the dispersing crowd. "Because Dad was an outlaw you hounded Johnny, said he was crooked and wild and would never amount to much. You wouldn't let him live like a normal man on the range that reared him. This riding job with Brad Gulistan was his first break."

Reed's head dropped a notch and he felt the hot sting of remorse.

"I'm sorry, Ma'am, that it had to be Johnny that died and me that killed him."

"Sorry!" she flared. A hint of unruliness touched her features. "You're nothing but a two-bit gunman. I can see it in your eyes, in the way you talk and hold yourself. Now that you're here I suppose you'll pitch into the range war and hire out your holsters to the highest bidder."

"Is that all?" Reed asked quietly.

Conflicting thoughts and emotions simmered in his brain. He was thinking how anger and scorn intensified the stormy beauty of this girl. There was a strange excitement in him and her nearness was like a soft, singing wind brushing against his senses.

Reed's life was a life that ran in intricate and lonely channels with danger for his saddle mate. There had never been any place for a woman in his stern existence. Yet, watching the lamplight bring out the golden richness in Sally Drennan's hair, seeing the grace of her slender body, the fullness of her lips filled him with an odd and elusive regret.

But she was not through with him. Grief had made her stiffly wretched and now she had a rough desire to hurt this dark and solid and implacable man.

"Not quite all," she responded. "You may find yourself not as tough as you think. This is a hard, unfriendly land. It may have a bullet for you—with your name on it."

Reed did not move. His face was impassive, but he never stopped looking at her.

"You may be right," he agreed. "But that bullet will have to find me first. When it does, it's likely to meet another going the other way."

For a long interval their eyes held across the distance and she was the first to turn away.

"Ben," she said to the sheriff. "Will you see that Johnny's body is removed to Syl Cogan's undertaking parlor?"

"Sure thing, Sally," the lawman replied. "Couple of you men, lend me a hand right now."

Reed's troubled gaze continued to watch Sally Drennan. He had killed before—although only for a good reason and when there was no other course open to him—but somehow he realized that he would never be able to forget the shooting of Johnny Drennan. The memory of Sally, torn by her grief, yet locking that grief irrevocably within her, would go down the trail with him and it would leave him no peace.

It was at times like these that he found a terrible distaste for his job. Moving in a hard world that gave no quarter, he had schooled himself to expect no mercy and to show none in return. Too often it was kill or be killed. Yet, up to this moment his strength, his fearlessness had helped him to survive where others had died. But in surviving he had lost something. Life had driven the gentleness out of him, leaving no room for laughter.

Now he swung slowly about. He let his long-barreled Colt slide back into its leather sheath. He walked diagonally across the street then, his boots making a solid beat of sound on the packed earth.

3

AT the Antlers Hotel he turned from the plank sidewalk and strode into the deserted lobby. A scrawny, pale-eyed clerk got up from a rough-hewn chair, threw down a mail order catalogue he had been reading, and ducked behind the board partition which served as a counter.

A board on the rear wall was studded with nails from which dangled a ponderous array of room keys.

"I want a room," Reed said.

The clerk grabbed the thumb-scored register, placed it in front of Reed and handed him a pen. Below the last entry Reed wrote three words:

Jim Reed, Cheyenne

"Room sixteen," murmured the clerk, his eyes furtively probing Reed. From the board behind him he took a rusty key and passed it to Reed, afterward entering the room number beside Reed's name.

Reed climbed a flight of rickety stairs to the second floor. He traversed a gloomy corridor to its end and found number sixteen to be the last room, facing the rear street behind the hotel. Inside he lit a lamp on the battered table by the window, then stepped rapidly away from it. Afterward, he let his glance wander around the chamber.

It was bare and plain and stuffy with the day's heat. A spur-scarred iron bed stood in the center. There were two straight-backed chairs, a dusty calendar tacked on the wall, one table on which the lamp rested, and another table set beneath a cracked mirror. On this second table reposed a deep bowl and a pitcher half-filled with water.

It was like every other room in every other hotel in every other cowtown he had visited. There was nothing here to hold a man, except the weariness produced by hours spent on the trail and the need for sleep—and a man slept better under the stars with his saddle for a pillow, the good earth for his bed and the sage-scented night air for his trail-mate. But there was a job to be done in Outpost and so he would stay and watch and wait.

He took off his dusty shirt, poured some water from the pitcher into the bowl and washed the dirt and grime from his hands and face. Then, feeling refreshed, he slipped on the same shirt and went downstairs, crossing the street to the barber shop. There he got a haircut and had a two days' growth of beard shaved from his face.

Supper hour was well past when he emerged into Outpost's main street again. From somewhere down the street came the clink of glasses, the tinny clangor of a piano, the harsh laughter of men, then the shrill peal of woman's voice. Outpost's night life was building up. Cowhands from nearby outfits were riding in, looping their reins around the tie rail, before tramping into the saloons.

Reed felt the need of a drink to wash the trail dirt out of his throat, but he pushed the thought aside and walked back to the hotel. Halfway across the street, he saw a man's idle shape posed in the dark maw of the livery stable. He caught the winking red eye of a cigarette stub arcing through the dust. The man turned once to regard Reed, then strode away into the gloom.

Pressure rippled along Reed's shoulders. Once again he was reminded that he was a stranger in a hostile town. There was no trust in any of these men. They would be wondering now what business brought him here, and that would give them no rest until he had declared himself. Meanwhile, he had already made some enemies and his back was a broad and sure target for any man who was in the mood for back-shooting.

But no shot came and the prickling sensation left the nape of his neck. A glance showed him that the hotel dining room was still open, so he strolled in through the lobby and took a corner table that allowed him a full view of the empty room.

The waitress took his order for steak and potatoes. When she returned he began eating with a relish that surprised himself. Halfway through the meal Brad Gulistan entered and came directly across the room to him.

A thin crease appeared between Reed's narrowed eyes. Involuntarily his glance centered on a broad welt plastered against the left-hand curve of Gulistan's jawline. Gulistan saw that glance and flushed.

Reed set his knife and fork down as Gulistan reached the table. He was cool and serene and his face mirrored no emotion—not even curiosity—yet all his muscles were pressing against his skin and he had his legs solidly braced under the chair.

"What do you want?" Reed demanded surlily.

"Talk," said Gulistan.

Reed took time to study Gulistan.

"Go ahead."

Gulistan pulled a chair out from the table and sat down facing Reed, his back to the hotel lobby.

"Are you a nervous man?" Reed asked quietly.

"What are you gettin' at?"

Reed looked beyond Gulistan. The latter turned to follow Reed's gaze. Two tall, hard-eyed hands from Gulistan's Circle G spread lounged in the doorway.

"It's all right, boys," said Gulistan. "Wait for me outside."

The two punchers looked at one another, shrugged and drifted away. Gulistan swung his attention back to Reed and smiled, his long lips imparting a careful, shrewd quality to the gesture.

"I may have been mistaken about you, Reed. I watched you before. You've got sand and you don't back down easy."

"You sing a different tune," observed Reed.

"Yeah. A man can misjudge another," Gulistan was affable, his voice confidential. "How would you like to work on the Circle G?"

"You hiring cowhands or gunhands?"

"What do you think?" Gulistan's flat lips spread in a grin. He took his careful, deliberate look at Reed, studying his solid shoulders, his powerful arms. "You look like a man who is friendly with his gun. I can use someone like that. The pay is ninety a month and found."

"That's good money."

"Sure, but the right man would be worth it."

Reed showed the rancher only a speculative curiosity so Gulistan plunged on doggedly.

"I don't know what brought you here and I don't care. You probably heard enough tonight to know that we're having trouble on this range. Cattle have been rustled; line fences cut; night riders shot from ambush.

"Jack Braley and his gang of outlaws have

32

been seen on the edge of the badlands. It's a cinch someone here is working with them. Harry Wright and some of his friends think I'm the man. And Johnny Drennan turning stage bandit didn't help my cause. I'm telling you now I'm not the person behind those raids."

"But it could be Harry Wright?" asked Reed softly.

Temper flared in Gulistan and he scowled.

"Yeah, it could be, but there's no proof," he replied gruffly. "We've all lost beef and some of us are pooling our herds for a drive to railhead at Halton, the town beyond Estreva. Once we ship some steers to Eastern markets we may be able to collect enough cash to pay off our notes. Another big raid would ruin me. I'm backed to the wall now and Clark Esmond, the banker, won't give any extensions.

"I've even thought Esmond might be to blame. He holds notes on almost every outfit in Outpost. If he were to foreclose on all the big spreads, he could be a cattle baron, the likes of which the West has never seen."

"So you're hiring gun hands to hold onto your range?"

"That's right." Savagery pinched Gulistan's features. He was a big, vital man with deep-

33

seated feelings and not much patience. "You saw some of my crew. They're hard-cases. I want them that way. You're of the same breed. There'll be more trouble. When it comes I hope to be ready for it and God help the man who is doublecrossin' his neighbors." He paused, shoved back his chair and stood up. "What do you say?"

Reed's manner was irritatingly calm, his answer unhurried.

"I'll think about it."

Something dark and dubious came into Gulistan's heavy face.

"There's a range war brewing, Reed. If you aim to stay in Outpost, you'd better be sure you're on the right side."

"Which is the right side?"

Gulistan's temper slipped. Grim lines bracketed his mouth.

"Hell, I've wasted enough time with you!" he declared. "If you want the job ride out to see me tomorrow at the Circle G." His eyes narrowed and his voice turned harsh. "But get this. If the answer is no, stay out of my way. You bucked me once. Don't try it again if you want to live."

Reed kicked his chair free and stood up. He

plunged his hand into a pocket and tossed two silver dollars on the table.

"I make my own decisions," he said, looking straight at the cowman, "and nobody will bluff me." A thin muscle throbbed in his jaw. There was something inflexible, unrelenting in his manner and during the brief interval that Reed paused, strain built up a nagging pressure in the room. "If I buy cards in this range war, I'll play them as I see them. If the cards call for me to buck a man, I'll buck him. And that man can be you or anyone else. It would make no difference to me."

Gulistan's shoulders shook with suppressed fury. He was a big man in Outpost and he was not accustomed to opposition. He experienced a hard moment during which he forced himself to swallow his rage, then he turned away.

Reed followed and the two men marched through the lobby. Out at the edge of the walk one of the hard-faced punchers who had been lounging in the doorway of the dining room ran up. His talk beat at Gulistan and excitement broke through the reserve on his cheeks.

"Brad, Tom Jackson wants to see you. He says it's important."

"Yeah? Where is Jackson?"

"In the back room of the Second Chance Saloon."

Gulistan shrugged and swung off along the walk. Reed remained motionless. He saw the puncher talking to Gulistan, tugging at the rancher's thick arm, and once the man swung his head around to fling a tense, excited glance toward Reed.

An odd restlessness whipped through Reed. Finally he spun across and reentered the hotel, moving wearily across the lobby.

Upstairs in his room he lit the lamp once more and drew the blind on the single window that overlooked a rear alley. A lean-to shed was attached to the hotel, the slanting roof coming within four feet of the window. Beyond the shed was a barn and he could hear a few horses stamping restlessly in the enclosure.

Locking the door, his right hand moved mechanically toward the pocket of his shirt, probing for his deputy U. S. marshal's badge, and found the pocket empty. Uneasiness crawled through his mind when a complete search of his clothes proved futile.

He remembered having felt the badge in his pocket before the raid on the stage. Accordingly, it must have dropped out in the struggle with Drennan in the stage or had fallen in the dust when he had bent to lift up the dying stage driver's body.

No doubt the badge had been found, either inside the stage or in the street, and it would not take long for the finder to put facts and impressions together and decide the identity of its owner.

Losing that badge was an unfortunate break. It might easily complicate his task here. Should the badge fall into the possession of the wrong parties it would tip Reed's hand, bring him definitely into the open, mark him for destruction. For it had occurred to him that men who were ruthless enough to rustle beef and commit cold-blooded killings would not hesitate to dispose of a lone lawman who might interfere with their plans.

All the roughness returned to Reed's countenance now and he was thinking of Marshal Bill Zane, his superior at Cheyenne. Old Bill had called him into his office four days ago and by the set lines bracketing the marshal's cheeks, Reed had known there was another trouble trail to be followed.

"Jim," Zane had said, coming right to the point, "there's a job waiting for you in Outpost.

37

It's the old story of a range war building. Cattle are being rustled, line riders killed."

Zane had gone on to paint the entire picture —the impending clash between Gulistan's Circle G and Wright's Slash W outfit, and the rumors about Jack Braley's wild bunch.

"It's a job for half a dozen marshals," Zane had admitted. "But you know how it is. We don't have enough men to go around so you'll have to tackle it alone."

"Better that way," was all Reed had said.

"Yeah. You always did prefer to lone-wolf it, but it doesn't make your job any easier. You'll be going into a hostile land, Jim, where no man will be your friend, where your badge won't be any protection. I'll leave it up to you whether you work in the open or under cover—but do the job and report back to me."

That had been four days ago. Now Reed was in Outpost and already he had killed one man, and the feeling was strong within him that this was only the beginning.

Finally Reed shrugged his thoughts aside, unbuckled his cartridge belt, looped belt and holster around a bed post and dropped, fully clothed, upon the bed.

The rigors of four days' travel had taken a

toll of his energy, and sleep was a powerful urge in his body.

How long he slept he did not know. But he suddenly found himself wide awake in a room that was hot and dark and thoroughly alive with the threat of peril.

There was a taut dryness in his throat and he knew at once that someone was in the room. For the space of five long seconds during which time the blood seemed to pump through his veins with the loud beat of a tom-tom Reed's eyes tried to penetrate the gloom.

The blind was up, and now he distinctly recalled pulling it down before retiring. A board creaked near the foot of the bed. Someone's breathing rasped faintly in the silence. Then Reed saw the grayness of the window turn black and he realized a man had moved in front of it.

Slowly and carefully he braced himself on his elbows. Then a dark figure leaped up from behind the foot of the bed and hurtled toward him.

Reed swung his legs to the floor, feeling the man's shape slide past him, hearing the strike of knife steel on a bed post. The man cursed and Reed hit him below the knees with his on-driving shoulder. The knife slashed wildly through space. It ripped Reed's shirt near the neck, just grazing the flesh. Reed lashed out, flinging all of his weight upon his attacker, both hands gripping the man's knife wrist and twisting it with a savage strength.

"Luke, where are you?" hissed the man by the window.

No answer followed that tense question. Reed exerted more pressure on his assailant's wrist, felt the grip relax. Then the knife slid to the floor with a dull clatter. Reed rammed his fist into the man's face and rose to meet the second man's charge. A blow caught Reed in the Adam's apple. Gagging for breath, he toppled over backwards. The base of his skull struck a leg of the bed. Pain punished him in throbbing waves and a dull roaring sounded in his ears.

He pulled himself to his feet. A thick body careened against him. He shoved the man away with the palms of his hands, then hit him solidly with a right and left to the face. A sobbing breath rasped from tortured lungs, then welted knuckles struck Reed in the mouth. He swung again, missing widely and staggered from a blow to the jaw.

"Stand away, Luke!" growled the man near Reed.

Steel scuffed against holster leather and Reed knew the speaker was drawing a gun. He experienced a hopeless moment during which he thought about his own weapon draped over a bedpost. Then he drove forward low and hard as a gun roared almost in his face. A ruddy tongue of flame flickered past him, the bullet tearing into the wall behind his left shoulder.

"Ace, you damned fool!" bellowed the man called Luke. "The boss said no shootin'!"

Then Reed was in close and grappling with the man who held the gun, fighting to disarm him. The gun went off twice more, the slugs slamming into the floor, before Reed forced the man to drop it. Now both attackers closed in upon him and all three moved across the boards in a threshing tangle. They tripped over a table, carrying it with them to the floor.

A thumb gouged at Reed's eye. A knuckled fist jammed against his mouth and blood ran warmly around his teeth. It was wicked, punishing battling with no holds barred. A knee drove into middle of Reed's back. The blow brought sharp, excruciating pain. He rolled to one side as the man beneath him locked an arm around his neck.

Rapidly that muscled arm tightened, cutting

off Reed's breathing. He felt the hot blood rushing up to his head and agony slashed at his lungs. He was dimly aware of boots pounding up the stairs.

"Luke, finish him!" screamed the man who was trying to throttle Reed. "Where's your knife?"

The cold hand of death was a cruel vise, squeezing at Reed's heart. The veins in his neck were like thick cables, throbbing and trembling while that arm about his windpipe increased his pressure. In sheer desperation he punched his elbow into the throat of the man above him, heard the fellow rasp and roll clear.

Reed twisted swiftly, got his hands on the arm of the man beneath him. His steel-like fingers crept down to the wrist, found a hold there. With blackness crowding in over his mind he dug his fingers into the nerve centers of the man's wrist until the arm jerked away.

Reed wrenched to one side as the other man renewed the fight, jumping upon him. Tough and hard as he was, Reed had taken a beating. It occurred to him that he must win this unequal fight in the next few minutes or he would never survive.

The boots pounding up the stairs came

stamping down the corridor. A fist rattled the door panels and a voice boomed.

"Open up in there before we break the door down!"

Reed paid no attention to that summons. He was on his back now and the other man was questing for a stranglehold again. Rough fingers clawed for Reed's throat. They found their mark, but Reed's knees shot up and outward, catching his attacker in the pit of the belly and catapulting him halfway across the room.

Glancing toward the gray gloom of the window, Reed saw the dark blot of the other man's shape close upon him. A booted foot jolted into his side. A knee bit his chin, closing his mouth with a snap that threatened to ram his teeth into his gums.

He was flung backwards and brought up against the wall. The man came at him, but he rolled clear, clambered to his feet. For a moment, then, they stood upright, trading savage punches in the darkness, the only sound the long pull of their labored breathing.

Reed hit his man with two solid rights to the jaw, saw the man retreat, come up against the table that held the water pitcher. Reed charged forward, anticipating the next move and ducking as the pitcher swept past him to splinter on the floor.

The other man struck at him with a chair, the rungs sliding along the edge of his shoulder. Yonder, the pounding on the door increased and someone's heavy weight was thrown against the panels.

Reed tripped over the splintered chair, fell against the man nearest the window. A wild blow raked Reed's chin. Then he put his head against the man's chest, ripped an uppercut to the jaw that propelled the man halfway through the window. The man uttered one shrill yell.

"Come on, Luke!"

Then Reed saw the man careen through the opening and bounce to the shed, afterward scrambling hastily down the sloping shed roof. A door panel splintered as the men outside tried to batter it down. Reed whirled to grapple with Luke. A gun butt grazed the side of his head and he felt dizziness drop like a cloak upon his mind.

He flung out his arms, got them around his attacker. The gun descended again. Reed was growing weaker, but he set his teeth against the pain. His arms tightened around the other man and he heaved upward, lifting the man off the floor and hurtling him against the wall.

A strangled breath broke from the man. Plaster showered down when his body struck. Then the floor shook to the solid thump of his fall. At the same instant the door crashed inward under the impact of driving shoulders.

A man plunged through, toppled on his face, then climbed rapidly to his feet. Behind him charged several others. Reed swung his attention that way, his bruised, knuckle-roughened cheeks clearly outlined in the yellowish glare of a storm lantern held by the hotel clerk.

The excited babble of voices broke through a brief straining silence. Then Sheriff Ben Collier, looking sleepy-eyed and incongruous in his nightshirt which he had tucked into his black pants, thrust forward with a gun in his hand.

"Stand hitched, Reed!" he growled. "I've got you covered."

Reed's lips flattened against his teeth. There was a livid bruise under his left eye, a shallow cut on his lip. His shirt was torn in two places and blood made a dark, sticky stain above the knife wound in his shoulder which now began to ache dully.

"Better watch him, Collier!" urged a tall,

thin man who stood behind the sheriff. "I heard shooting."

"Sure you did," said Reed, the gray pallor of exhaustion pinching his features. "And I was the man being shot at. If you're worried, Collier, there's my gun still in its holster on the bed. It hasn't been fired."

The hotel clerk held the lantern high, throwing a shaft of light against the far wall where the fight had ended up. His eyes widened with shock.

"Gosh, it's Luke Stacey!"

Reed's bleak-eyed gaze, traveling to his attacker, narrowed and a fatal remorse hit him. The man he had thrown against the wall lay limp and utterly unmoving. His cheeks were gray and battered and still. Looking at him, Reed knew the man would never fight again. His body was wedged against the wall, the neck grotesquely twisted and broken.

"Luke Stacey!" the thin man repeated slowly. "One of Harry Wright's hands."

Reed's attention turned thin and sharp at this announcement. He looked up at the thin man, his mind a seething tumult.

The sheriff walked past Reed and had his grim, silent look at Stacey. Afterward, he wheeled around, shook his head with a dismal fatalism and approached the bed. Removing Reed's gun from the holster, he broke it open, spun the cylinder, and lifted the barrel to his nostrils. All this while Reed never moved and his face was like granite.

"Friend," said the sheriff, watching Reed intently, "trouble seems to follow you around."

"And wherever he goes he leaves a dead man," added the thin man, his pale blue eyes hostile. "First it was Drennan and now Stacey."

"You've got a lot to say," Reed observed. "Who are you?"

"He's Clark Esmond," Ben Collier broke in quickly. "Owner of the Outpost bank. I picked him up on my way here after the clerk roused me down at the jail tellin' me there was a ruckus in the hotel. Esmond was just leavin' the Stockmen's Saloon."

Reed's shoulders stirred restlessly. When he tipped his head to stare at the floor dizziness flowed over him. Patiently he waited for his vision to focus.

"You keep late hours for a banker," Reed said.

"Hell, sheriff. Are we goin' to stand here and jaw all night?" somebody in the hall murmured.

47

"You feel like talkin' about it, Reed?" Collier asked gruffly.

"There were two of them," Reed said tersely. "I'd been sleepin' soundly. I woke up suddenly and knew someone was in the room. As I moved out of bed both men jumped me. One of them escaped out the window—the way they came in—when you started smashin' down the door. The other fellow wasn't so lucky."

"You put it mildly," said Collier.

Reed gazed at Stacey. A faint distaste for his entire business ridged his mouth.

"I'm sorry Stacey is dead," he resumed. His somber thoughts kept drawing down the lids of his eyes, putting a hard glint in their slate-gray depths for every man to see. "I was hopin' to make him talk."

"It appears somebody wants to see you dead," the sheriff said, his seamed face thoughtful. "Any idea why?"

"Your guess is as good as mine."

"You've only been in town a few hours yet you've made enemies. Why would one of Wright's waddies want to kill you?"

"I don't know but I can find out."

"Collier," said Esmond, "take my advice and

lock this man up until we learn more about him. Find out what his business is."

"It's none of yours," snapped Reed.

The banker stiffened. His mouth turned distinctly unpleasant. He was built like a rail fence without an ounce of fat on him. His face was inordinately pale and the tight flesh of his cheekbones made distinct hollows beneath the jutting shelf of the protruding bones.

"You tell a pat story," he said. "It's your word against—"

"Stacey's?" finished Reed with a dry, humorless smile. "And he isn't talkin'."

Collier shook his head warily.

"Don't get any crazy ideas, Esmond," he warned. "I'll handle this my way. Reed's tellin' the truth as I see it. My duty is to have a talk with Wright in the morning."

"Get up early, Sheriff, if you want to be there ahead of me," Reed informed him grimly.

Collier holstered his gun and spoke tartly.

"Stay clear of that outfit. I want no more killings."

"Neither do I. But if there's to be any, I don't intend to be on the receivin' end."

Collier looked at him. The sheriff was a dogged, plodding sort of man. He had his

49

scruples, his stern sense of duty but something about Jim Reed made him a little uncertain of his ground.

"There's a range war buildin' here," he said. "It'll be dog eat dog. Which side you on?"

"Who said I was takin' sides?" Reed demanded.

"You can't stay on the fence."

"We'll see."

Anger ruffled Collier's feelings. He straightened and the slight stoop left his shoulders. Now he turned on the crowd and took his displeasure out upon them.

"Get out of here, all of you!" he growled. "The fight's over."

Men grumbled among themselves and slowly began drifting down the corridor toward the stairs, leaving just Collier, Esmond, the hotel clerk and Reed inside the room.

"You're in the clear, Reed," said Collier. "But from now on I'm watching you mighty close. Stay away from Harry Wright."

"No. I handle my own affairs. Stacey was gunnin' for me. Maybe he had orders from Wright. I mean to find out."

50

4

THE sun had already climbed above the serrated peaks when Jim Reed pushed his hired bay gelding along the winding wagon road that traveled westward out of Outpost. The hills were thickly timbered, with here and there broad, grassy meadows forming a green oasis in the hollows.

Behind him were the rocky ridges of the Royuna range. Ahead loomed the rugged battlements of the far-flung badlands. But here, following the road in this tremendous valley between the two great mountain ranges, was ideal cattle land.

Three miles out of Outpost he topped a low knoll that overlooked Jack Payson's small Sombrero ranch. With the detailed map old Bill Zane had given him, he was able to identify all the outfits. A small herd of cattle grazed the slopes near Payson's run-down ranch buildings.

Within the next half hour Reed passed three more shoestring spreads. Two of them were

51

watered by small creeks that made a crystal glitter against the green carpet of grass.

There was a dull ache in Reed's bones from last night's fight and his shoulder where the knife blade had penetrated the flesh was stiff and sore. Some of the welts and bruises on his face had turned to a blue-green color and his upper lip was slightly swollen.

Before him now the road rose steadily, the grades becoming steeper, the timber thicker. Yet, oddly enough, the meadows here in the higher country were broad and well watered. In the distance he discerned large herds of cattle and an occasional rider.

A line fence angled down a steep slope and continued on out of sight through a wide belt of pines and alders. Reed knew from his map that this fence divided the extensive range governed by Brad Gulistan and Harry Wright, the two largest cattle barons in Outpost.

Reaching a fork in the road, Reed took the right branch and headed for a dim cluster of buildings nestling in a grassy draw.

The hot glare of the sun made Reed tip his hat lower over his tanned face. But his eyes missed nothing and registered all the tiny landmarks, the hills, the watercourses and timbered areas with a careful attention. And all the while he rode the dull beat of the bay's hoofs on the hard-packed dirt was a dull accompaniment to the somber turn of his reflections.

He was thinking of his lost deputy marshal's badge and the attack upon him in the hotel room. That attack was proof enough that he was a marked man in Outpost. But for whom? There was Gulistan's early antagonism, his paradoxical change of tune and the indisputable fact that Johnny Drennan was a Gulistan hand —all of which pointed to the Circle G owner as the man who should be watched.

Yet, he could not discount Harry Wright or the circumstance that it was Stacey, a Slash W puncher, who had tried to kill him in the hotel. On the face of it that could mean that Wright had found his, Reed's, badge and had moved at once to dispose of Reed as a hazard to his outlaw enterprise. Either man—Gulistan or Wright—had motive enough to go outside the law for wealth and power.

In addition to Outpost's two leading ranchers, there were two other men who came under Reed's attention—Val Ormand, the stageline owner, and Clark Esmond, the banker. He had to admit to himself that he had not the slightest shred of evidence to suggest anything off-color in their dealings. Yet, he was fully aware that stage owners had been known to help rob their own insured shipments, and bankers had been known to join forces with renegade elements to hasten the ruin of cattlemen whose property was mortgaged to the bank.

Perhaps it was Esmond who was inciting the range trouble—who had hired Stacey and another man to dispose of Reed. For, it was not too incredible that a man should serve more than one master, or that Stacey, drawing his pay from the Slash W, might also be long-looping for another boss on the side.

The more he considered Clark Esmond as a suspect the more he was inclined to discount him. But the many risks of Reed's past had taught him never to overlook a single possibility. This much was certain, however. The man or men he sought knew his identity and what his mission in Outpost was. And so he could expect that whoever had ordered his death would try again. It was a pattern that was always repeated, an evil mob that would destroy him unless he destroyed first.

These were his thoughts, this was the challenge awaiting him as he pointed the bay down a gentle slope, entering an avenue of trees that led directly to the Slash W ranch buildings. But the only effect on Reed was the swift, sure upheaval of the wildness in his nature. And so though the way ahead be dark and uncertain he would welcome each obstacle or hazard with a confidence born in his own fierce strength.

Reed came to the end of the lane and halted in front of the broad veranda. He saw the stocky figure of Harry Wright rise from a straight-backed chair in the shadows and stride to the top step of the porch.

"Climb down," invited Wright. His eyes were bland and watchful.

"Thanks," replied Reed. "I'll stay in the saddle."

Reed spoke pleasantly, with no hint of insolence, yet he knew that Wright was affronted. In cattle country, if a man was not invited to dismount he had his immediate notice that he was unwelcome. In a similar manner a man who was asked to get down and refused, showed by that action that his intentions were not friendly.

Now Wright came heavily down the steps. He moved to within ten feet of the bay and his glance was surly. Reed noticed it and calmly let his attentions drift across the yard to study each of the buildings.

Cottonwoods surrounded the ranchhouse, providing wide patches of shade. Somewhere in the rear he could hear the musical babble of a creek brawling over shallows. A hundred yards to the left on a slight knoll there was a long log bunkhouse. Nearby was an unpainted barn with assorted riding gear strewn on the ground. And off behind the house he could see a corner of the peeled pole corral with a cavvy of unsaddled horses raising a fine gray dust within the enclosure.

"You here on business or just ridin'?" Wright wanted to know.

Three punchers strolled out of the bunkhouse and spread out around Reed, their hands hovering close to their guns.

"Business," said Reed slowly.

He lifted his eyes beyond Wright when the door opened and a girl and another man stepped onto the veranda. The girl came forward, stopping at the railing. Reed had a full glimpse of her dark, sleek hair, the regal, almost patrician turn of her cheeks. She was tall and slender, her body firmly molded in a tight-bodiced blue dress with a white frilly collar and a long skirt.

Her long-lashed hazel eyes studied Reed boldly and her mouth was very close to a smile.

The thick-bodied, deep-chested man beside her noticed the change in the girl's face and scowled.

"It's customary to introduce guests, Father," the girl reminded Wright softly.

"I'm not sure if he is a guest."

"But isn't he the man you spoke about? From your description—"

"All right, Diana," Wright growled while the thick-bodied man exhibited a growing irritation. "Reed, this is my daughter, Diana. The man beside her is my foreman, Noel Hockett."

Reed removed his hat and smiled.

"My pleasure, Ma'am," he murmured, the smile doing something to his face, relaxing its tough, hard cast. He nodded to Hockett.

Hockett grunted something unintelligible, but Diana Wright gave Reed the full impact of her expressive eyes. He was immediately aware that here was a woman with the power to move men, to disturb their thinking and arouse their emotions. There was wilfulness and pride in the thrust of her chin. She was sure of herself and quite conscious of her charms.

"Well, Father, why are you hesitating?"

Diana prodded. "If this man really bluffed Brad Gulistan out of a gunfight last night I should think you could use him. You know we haven't had much success in trailing the rustlers who have been stealing from us. Don't forget we lost another three hundred head two nights ago and that trail led to the badlands, then petered out."

"Stay out of this, Diana," grunted Hockett.

The foreman's ruddy face was mottled by anger. He had deep blue eyes, a little narrow and a little hard. His hair was blond and short-cropped beneath a battered gray sombrero.

Diana frowned at Hockett, took a step away from him. Again her eyes, warm, and provocative and compelling, traveled to Reed.

"All right," snapped Wright. He shrugged his shoulders. "We've had plenty of trouble, Reed. There's a job here for you—if you want it."

"We're not that short of hands that we have to hire strange gunslicks," growled Hockett.

Reed looked up. He saw how Hockett's lips were flaring against his yellowed teeth. A natural antagonism had sprung up between the two men. It was as real and as solid as a canyon wall. Reed was aware of the reason for the ramrod's resentment. There was a strong desire in Noel Hockett—a hunger for Diana Wright. It showed in his eyes which seldom left the girl, and in the roughness of his talk to Reed.

"You hirin' gunmen, too?" Reed inquired.

"What do you mean—too?" demanded Wright. An uneasy silence rolled across the yard before the cowman added: "You had other offers?"

"Maybe."

"You don't have to tell me. It was Brad Gulistan." Swift distaste darkened Wright's face. "You playin' both ends against the middle?"

Before Reed could answer Diana broke in, a mocking note in her voice and a sly smile in her eyes for Reed.

"Why no, Father. Maybe he's just looking for the highest bidder. A man that hires out his guns has to get the most the traffic will bear."

Reed said nothing. Only his eyes flickered strangely. A low curse broke from Hockett and he tramped down the veranda steps. The sun glinted on the shells in his gunbelt, and there was an arrogant swagger to his stride. Now Wright moved closer to Reed and the other three hands began to slide their boots through

59

the yard's dry dust. Suddenly the tension in the air was thick enough to cut.

"Ride on, Reed. Ride on," growled Wright. "I'll do no bidding against Gulistan or any other man for a gunslick. If you hire out to Gulistan, stay off my land or you'll be fair game." He broke off and suspicion built up a hot brightness in his eyes. "My friend, you wouldn't be a marshal, would you?"

Reed remained straight and motionless in the saddle. His face showed no change of expression, but nerve pressure was like a thick fog in his mind. Was this what he had waited for? And was Wright his man?

Warning stirred through him, knotting the muscles in his stomach, quickening the run of his breathing.

"That's a strange question," he said.

"A strange question for a strange man," Wright declared.

"Did you send Luke Stacey to ask me that last night?" Reed demanded softly and ominously.

"Stacey?" Wright's question was guarded and uncertain.

"You had a cowhand named Stacey, didn't you?"

"*Had?*"

"I mean he's dead."

"Wait a minute!" blurted Hockett. His beet-red face flushed to a deeper hue. "How do you know that? Talk fast, mister."

"He tried to kill me last night in the hotel," Reed's voice sank to a lower, deadlier pitch. "He and another man. His partner got away. I figure a man always kills for a reason. Stacey must have had a reason. Maybe you're it."

A lean hardness whipped into the cattle owner's cheeks. A gray pallor touched the hinge of his jaw and a vein along the side of his neck began to throb like a charged electric cable.

"Reed, if you finished Stacey, you've signed your own death warrant." Wright spoke hoarsely. "Stacey had orders to stick in my north line cabin to watch a beef herd grazin' my upper pasture."

"It seems he didn't stay there," Reed told him.

Hockett's right arm dropped to hang his spread hand like a greedy claw above his holstered gun. Behind Reed the others stiffened.

"The air has turned sour since Reed rode in," stated Hockett. "I don't know what brings him

61

here but if Stacey is dead then the only way Reed leaves here is feet first."

Hockett was teetering on the verge of a break. Wildness began to fan a torrid glow in Reed's chest and the raw taste of violence was once more in his mouth. Abruptly he kicked the bay in the ribs, and plunged the animal against Wright. His gun leaped into his fist and lined on the rancher. Behind him Reed heard metal rasp against leather, heard the nervous scraping of boots and he spoke tonelessly without turning.

"Go ahead, gents. My back is a big target for your guns. But remember this. The first man that shoots sends a bullet from my Colt into your boss."

Hockett took one step, then halted, his hand clenching and unclenching, his lips as rigid as an iron bar.

"Damn you, Reed."

Fear tugged at the corners of Wright's eyes.

"You play it rough," he murmured thickly.

"Only when the cards call for it," Reed told him.

Out of the corner of his eye Reed saw how color drained out of Diana's face as she carefully watched this scene.

"I guess it's your deal," growled Wright, cringing under the threat of Reed's gun bore. "But this game has some time to run. There'll be another deal, another hand. I'm thinkin' of Johnny Drennan and Luke Stacey. I'm thinkin' it may be Gulistan who paid you to down Stacey. And so it may be time to make a move against the Circle G."

"Don't do anythin' you might later regret," Reed warned. He remained somber and reflective a moment before going on. "There's somebody in this valley afraid I may find out too much. Whoever that man is, he wanted me out of the way. Stacey got the job. Stacey works for you. Maybe you gave him the orders."

Fury overcame Harry Wright's dread. He shouted at Reed.

"Get out or I'll take my chances."

"Sure, I'm goin'," said Reed and let his eyes lift toward a dust cloud boiling up along the distant wagon road. "In about ten minutes you're goin' to have a visitor. It'll most likely be Sheriff Ben Collier. He'll be wantin' to learn just how much you know about Stacey's attempt to gun me. I hope you have a good answer."

"What do you want us to do?" Hockett asked

Wright as desperation goaded him to the point of rashness.

"Here's what you'll do," Reed broke in promptly. "You'll stay where you are and Wright will walk out of the yard with me. I've got some ridin' to do. And if any of you feel like shootin' at my back why go ahead. It'll be tough on me—and Wright, too."

Reed spoke easily, yet there was a grim purpose in his manner that held the Slash W hands rigid and doubtful.

"Start walkin'," ordered Reed.

Wright glared balefully at him but obeyed. Hockett stepped reluctantly back to let him pass. Five hundred yards from the house Reed halted the rancher.

"Far enough. You can go back now."

"I'll see you again," Wright blurted savagely.

"Sure you will. Count on it."

Wright wheeled slowly and trudged off down the slope. When he was beyond gun range, Reed whirled the bay and set off at a fast run, striking northward in the direction of the badlands. He kept the bay to that steady pace for ten minutes, then pulled up along a wooded ridge to stare along his back-trail.

5

NO rising dust cloud puffed toward the sky so he knew that no pursuit had been organized at the Slash W. Nor had he expected any. Furious as Wright might be, his curiosity would impell him to wait and see what business brought that other rider jogging out from town.

Moving on again, Reed put the bay into a ground-eating canter, watching the land change shape and character before his eyes. The farther north he rode, the more rugged the terrain became. The gentle, rolling hills and grass-filled swales disappeared and he found himself in a region of high bluffs, twisting canyons, cutbank arroyos broken here and there by thickets of mesquite and ocotillo.

Yet, all along the narrow trail he followed he found unmistakeable evidence of the passage of cattle. He had picked up the sign a mile from Wright's northernmost patch of graze and he had immediately been reminded of Diana

Wright's revelation of a cattle theft two nights ago.

She had let it be known that the beef had not been recovered, that the trail had vanished in the labyrinthine wastelands. Because there had to be some explanation for the disappearance of large herds of cattle, Reed resolved to follow this sign to wherever it led. If he could find the answer to that riddle he might also have the answer to another puzzle. Who was behind the range trouble and who wanted him dead?

Sombrero tipped low over his craggy face to shield his eyes from sun-glare, he peered ahead through the shimmering heat waves. There was a welter of cattle and horse prints in the soft earth. Reed judged that the sign was two days old and he could see where a fresh band of riders had added their prints to the original sign left by the rustlers.

That second set of prints, of course, belonged to Wright's cowhands who had gone after the cattle.

Now a feeling of urgency crawled along Reed's nerves and he pushed the laboring bay forward at a swifter gait. Crossing a shallow arroyo, he moved along the western edge of a flat tableland almost lost in the deep shadows cast by the saw-toothed cliffs above.

At the far side of the broad plain the cattle and horse sign abruptly vanished. There was some evidence that a band of horsemen had milled about in indecision at the entrance of two canyons which joined at the edge of the tableland, but beyond that point there was nothing.

Riding a short distance up each canyon, Reed studied the hard, barren earth, seeking some clue that riders or cattle had passed in that direction but without any success. This, Reed decided, was ideal territory for rustlers. The ground was so hard and shaly that it would hold no hoof prints.

Back at the canyon forks he sat motionless in the saddle, putting his mind to the problem, yet unable to find any solution. A hot wind drilled down from the upper peaks, activating little whorls of dust which skidded down-canyon in a carefree, bouncing rhythm. Slowly, then, he lifted his eyes to the distant rim. He picked out a narrow twisting trail which clung to the south wall of the left-hand gorge like a thread clings to cloth.

By tortuous, switchback turns the trail

climbed steadily along the rocky facade. It would take a good horse to navigate the ascent and Reed was not sure of the bay gelding. However, some odd, nameless impulse moved him to have a try at it.

After the first three hundred yards the bay balked and started to buck, fighting the tug of the reins. But Reed's knees were like an iron vise upon the horse and he sat out the bay's ornery streak, afterward forcing the animal up the first steep pitch of the grade.

Now that he was actually negotiating the climb, he noticed that the ledge road was wider than it had appeared from the floor of the gorge. But all the way up he was hemmed in on one side by a jagged rock wall and on the other side by a sheer drop into empty space.

Reed had his moment of doubt in which he wondered at the wisdom of his maneuver, but the bay proved more sure-footed than he had expected him to be.

After twenty minutes of laborious going the bay angled out of the last switchback turn and trotted onto a high, boulder-strewn area.

Below Reed the gorge swam in shimmering heat waves, the brush and rocks dwarfed by distance. The wind was definitely stronger on the mesa, blowing in stiff, surging gusts.

For another half hour Reed continued aimlessly along the rim, his keen eyes cataloguing all the details of the high tableland. A mile away other peaks and buttes, higher than this upland mesa, lifted their massive summits toward the brassy sky.

He pulled up at last and swung to the ground to let the bay blow. Loosening the cinch, he ground-tied the animal, afterward stepping close to the rim to stare down into the canyon. At this point the gorge splayed out to a width of fifty feet and the brush grew more thickly along the bottom. Looking north, Reed noticed that the wide defile terminated in a wall of ruby-colored granite which towered two hundred feet above the mesa itself in a smooth-faced cliff to form the nucleus of another higher canyon beginning at the mesa's edge.

This odd rock formation shut off all possible view of what lay behind the new wall and in the V-like trough which Reed concluded must extend beyond the lower canyon's terminus. Below him, at the foot of the original gorge, a thick screen of chaparral made a rust-green back-drop against the expanse of gray granite.

He was staring at that screen of mesquite when half a dozen horsemen rode out of it, moving forward like dwarfed, toy figures through the heat haze.

Incredible as it seemed, there was a gap in the bluff behind the perfect concealment of chaparral. And that opening could only lead to the troughlike valley which must lie beyond the butte. Watching the slow, leisurely progress of those riders it occurred to Jim Reed that the hidden valley would be a perfect sanctuary for rustlers. Here must be the solution to the riddle of vanishing Outpost beef.

Although he had no idea what he might find beyond that canyon wall or how many men might be stationed there, nothing on earth could have kept Reed from having his look. And so he dropped behind a rocky outcropping and followed the horsemen with his intent gaze.

The horsemen proceeded steadily down-canyon, striking southward toward the lower hills. When it became difficult to follow their advance, Reed returned to his horse and back-tracked the way he had come, being careful not to let himself be skylined to the riders below.

He reached the narrow, winding trail that led to the bottom of the defile and again dismounted, waiting there until those yonder riders had passed from view. Then, reaching a swift decision, Reed put the bay down the treacherous descent. It was dangerous going, more precarious than the climb had been, but the bay picked its way accurately down the trail.

Cantering up-canyon toward the end of the gorge, Reed examined the shaly ground and found no marks of the passage of those riders save the occasional scrape of shod hoofs on rock which might have been missed by an ordinary hunter.

At last he reached the screen of brush which grew half-way up the side of the bluff. He had no idea what lay beyond the chaparral, but there was only one way to find out so he pushed the bay forward.

Dry, thorny bushes raked at Reed's face and dust filtered down upon him as the horse bucked the trees and shrubs. Seconds later he was out of the thorny tangle and riding in a dark, narrow defile. He proceeded for two hundred yards before the glen widened and sunlight threw its white brilliance upon an extensive valley completely hemmed in by rugged cliffs.

No matter in what direction he looked Reed saw wild peaks boxing in the valley with its lush, green areas of grassland. A creek made a bright glitter at the valley's north end, and in that direction he saw a faint spiral of smoke lift into the air.

Yonder there was a cabin. But at the moment it was hidden from his vision by a cluster of trees that formed a small park close against the canyon wall. About three hundred head of cattle were contentedly grazing along the grassy slopes a mile away.

Keeping to the brush that rimmed the pasture, he made a half-circle of the herd. Fifteen minutes later he came to the ashes of a branding fire. Running irons lay in the dirt and the ground was pock-marked by cattle and horse prints. Here, then, was where the rustlers blotted out original brands and substituted fresh brands before driving the steers across the state line.

Several longhorns drifted close to the edge of the brush and Reed noticed with a rising current of interest that two of them bore Harry Wright's Slash W markings. A clumsy attempt had been made to blur the brand and a Double

X had been burned into the animal's hide below it.

Two others carried Brad Gulistan's Circle G. Another bore a Dumbell brand. They were original markings and no attempt had yet been made to alter them.

Reed rode on, keeping to the brush until he had traversed the valley's entire width. At one point he had to cross a hundred yards in the open when the trees thinned out. But looking toward the cabin now visible through the pines of the base of the northwest bluff, he saw no sign of men.

Reaching the juncture of the north and west walls, his eyes sought another exit from the valley. Common sense told him these outlaws would be certain to provide themselves with a back door—another way out of their hiding place in the event of trouble. Moreover, the cattle had to be disposed of through some other exit save that by which they had entered.

Reed's eyes traveled all along the granite bluff. As far as he could see there was nothing but an endless line of cold, forbidding rock. But because he remembered the clever method by which the gateway to the valley from the south had been concealed, he pushed on, halting the bay finally in front of some chaparral whose odd, brownish color had attracted his attention. His eyes narrowed imperceptibly as he saw how it differed in hue from the rest of the surrounding brush.

Quickly he dismounted and grasped some of the bushes in his hands. They came out of the dry ground at the first hard tug. He realized, then, that they had been planted there to hide the V-like opening which pierced the cliff for a height of twenty feet. Yet, so thickly did the brush and saplings grow among the re-planted bushes that the cliff opening was invisible to anyone riding in the valley.

Reed went no farther, aware that the defile beyond led out of the valley, a perfect avenue of escape to other regions. Wheeling the bay around, he now angled back through the trees to approach the distant cabin on its blind side. For a brief interval he lost the cabin in the close-growing pines, but the smell of woodsmoke led him unerringly forward.

Fifty yards from the shack he dismounted. He left the bay ground-tied, loosened the long-barreled Colt in his holster and slid through the trees. He moved with the lithe stealth of the jungle cat and his nerves were primed for trouble.

The side wall of the cabin took shape before him. In a small clearing in the rear he saw a crude pole corral which held a cavvy of saddle horses. There was still no one in sight so he moved toward the nearest window. He took one long step out of the trees. Then a twig cracked behind him and a hard voice spoke at his elbow.

"Don't look now, brother, but there's somebody in back of you and he's got a gun."

6

THE frock-coated, dour-faced minister closed his worn, leather-bound Bible and the final words of his simple eulogy droned away into a sad, straining silence. His eyes lifted from the book, traveled to Sally Drennan, standing rigid and dry-eyed near the edge of the open grave.

There were deep shadows under her wide-spaced blue eyes and a little convulsion shook her shoulders which had become rounded at the points. She was a lonely, pathetic figure, her slender body outlined against the somber backdrop of rotting wooden headboards that marked other graves in Outpost's cemetery.

On a little knoll a short distance away lingered a host of curious onlookers from the town and nearby ranches. Val Ormand, Clark Esmond and Harry Wright stood apart, hats in their hands, watching this scene with a callous, unfeeling attention.

Esmond coughed, and the sound of it broke the uncomfortable stillness. There was in that idle gesture a vague urge to get this business over with, to get away from those bleak and barren surroundings.

Two laborers leaning on shovels near a mound of fresh earth let their eyes shuttle around questioningly to Sally Drennan. She met their gaze and nodded slowly.

"All right," she said in a husky whisper.

A faint ripple of relief seemed to roll over the crowd. The handful of men and women turned and directed their steps toward Outpost's main street a quarter of a mile away. The laborers slammed their shovels into the mound of dirt, facing about to fling the dry clods into the grave.

At this moment grief made its dull gray track across Sally's tanned features. If she could have cried, she might have found peace. But her turbulent emotions lay chained within her. This town was against her like it had been against her brother and her father before him—even like it had been against the hard-faced stranger, the man who had killed Johnny.

No compassion brought this crowd to Outpost's hill-top cemetery. Only cruel curiosity—a desire to see how she would take this blow to her normal existence, her thin hope for the future. With Johnny gone she was more alone than she had ever been.

But because this town waited to see her cry, watched for the break of her spirit, she hardened herself against them all. Despair was very real in her—like a hard vise around her heart—and unshed tears were a scalding inner tide, but her jaw thrust out in a gesture of defiance and she passed by them, white-lipped and stolid, going to her saddled horse.

Adjusting her brown, split-type riding skirt, her eyes were irresistibly drawn once more toward that gaping hole in the earth before she lifted herself into the saddle.

A rough, scaly hand was placed on her arm and she twisted about. The riding crop in her tight, round fist lifted threateningly, then fell limply to her side. Lance Koenig retreated a step. He fumbled awkwardly with his battered hat, his manner apologetic.

"My sympathies, Sally," he murmured.

She nodded, smiling with an obvious effort.

"You startled me," she explained, indicating her quirt.

"If there's anything I can do, let me know," the storekeeper reminded her. There was kindness in his pale cheeks and a tiny current of warmth sped through the girl.

"Thanks, Mr. Koenig. There's nothing. I'll be riding on."

Koenig bowed slightly and stepped side. Sally lifted the reins and cantered out of the aspen-logged cemetery gate. At the stage road she turned north away from town and put her mount into a swift gait, suddenly anxious to be alone.

She followed the road for three miles, then swung off at a narrow fork that angled across a steep grade for another half mile. At the bottom of another long ascent to a distant timbered ridge sprawled a two-room cabin. It was situated several hundred yards off the fork trail and a half dozen cottonwoods threw their generous pattern of shade about the yard. There were starched curtains at the front windows and a flower patch running along the east side.

Sally rode around to the rear, dismounting at the lean-to barn. She removed the saddle, bridle and blanket, hung the gear on a peg in the wall, then led her chestnut mare into the enclosure.

Walking past the vegetable patch she was reminded that she wanted to pick some beans for her lunch. But she had no heart for eating

79

at this moment and even the vivid display of flowers failed to penetrate her morose mood.

In the cabin's front room which Sally used as a combination kitchen and living room, she fussed a few moments at the sheet-iron stove, then moved to the desk against the far wall. Her fingers riffled through a sheaf of examination papers which had not yet been corrected.

She had them in her hands, staring at them yet not seeing them, when she heard the clatter of hoofbeats in the yard. Swiftly she dropped the test papers on the desk, strode to the door and flung it open. There was no smile of welcome on her face when Clark Esmond, Val Ormand and Harry Wright pulled up before her.

Esmond shoved his big Morgan horse forward. The animal's bigness dwarfed Esmond's slender thinness. He removed his hat with a flourish and the bony hollows of his cheeks became more pronounced when he smiled.

"Please accept our condolences," he said pompously.

Sally gestured impatiently with her hand. Her frosty eyes were unrelenting in their grief and bitterness.

"You didn't come here to tell me you were

sorry about Johnny," she told them bluntly. "You're glad he's dead. It's very plain to see. What brought you here? Come to the point."

A ripple of displeasure disturbed the careful suavity of Esmond's brown eyes. He grimaced angrily, but hesitated.

"Go ahead," urged Wright impatiently. "Tell her."

Sally stiffened. A dull pressure worked within her.

"It must be bad news," she said, "or three of you wouldn't have come along to watch and listen."

Esmond coughed in discomfort. His temper snapped and he let harshness creep into his voice.

"You're not very cordial," he stated. "I'll be the same. We have decided to call in a new school teacher for Outpost."

Esmond's talk whipped at Sally, flat and disturbing. Panic came momentarily into her face but she fought it down with desperation.

"So that's it," she murmured. Scorn colored her words. "You wasted no time in making a change. How could you refrain from giving me my notice in the cemetery?"

81

Esmond scowled, looked at Ormand and Wright. The stage owner remained dark and sleek and impassive. Harry Wright turned his face away, flushing to the roots of his gray-black hair.

"Aren't you being unfair?" he asked her finally.

"Unfair?" Sally repeated hotly. "You don't know the meaning of the word."

"Surely you can appreciate our position," Esmond remarked hastily. "After what happened to Johnny the town council met in special session. We decided that we couldn't risk having our children taught by a girl whose father and brother were—"

The banker broke off in obvious confusion.

"Outlaws," Sally finished.

"Yes," Esmond admitted. "We have nothing against you personally. It's just that talk does get around. Other towns will hear about Johnny just as they know about Blackjack Drennan, your father. There'll be gossip. It won't be nice and the welfare of our children is at stake, so we figured it wise to send for another teacher."

Sally Drennan felt her tiny world tumble into ruins. Bitterness was like a dry, gritty sand in her mouth. The heaviness around her heart increased.

"That's all I needed," she said dismally. Then her manner changed abruptly and she was angry again. "This must be a happy moment for all of you. None of you ever wanted me here. You kept me even though Dad lived outside the law because you couldn't get anyone else. You all hounded Johnny. You said that bad blood would tell. Well, if it did, it's because he never had a chance to live like other men."

She was shaking with anger and couldn't control that trembling and wouldn't control it even if she could.

"All right," she declared curtly. "You've said what you came to say. You can leave now. Or, are you waiting for my tears?"

"Hell, let's go," growled Harry Wright. "She's an unreasonable girl. We're wastin' our time here."

Esmond nodded, cursed under his breath and swung his horse around. Together, then, all three riders spurred their horses out of the yard.

7

JIM REED twisted slowly around, his hands lax and unmoving at his sides, facing toward the sound of the harsh voice that had challenged him. A dark, flat-featured man with a flaring nose and a knife-slash for a mouth stepped out of the trees behind him. There was a gun in the man's fist and the hammer was at full cock.

Pressure set up an uneasy tremor along Reed's nerves. He had to fight down an impulse to make a wild break for his own gun.

"You part of the welcomin' committee?" Reed inquired. His voice was scrupulously calm.

"You could call it that," said the other man. "I don't know how you found this valley, but it would have been better for you if you hadn't."

The gunman grinned at Reed. There was a wicked amusement in the gesture. Something turned over inside Reed's stomach. Without actually saying so in that many words, the gunman had given him a warning that he would soon be a dead man. Reed felt his horizon's close in upon him, felt the air become close and hard to breathe.

"How long do we stand here lookin' at each other?" he asked after a moment.

There was no cringe in his manner and none in his speech. It angered the gunman and he scowled, jabbing Reed in the back with his gun.

"Move around to the front of the cabin. The boss will want to see you."

The cabin door was ajar so Reed kicked it open and tramped inside, the gunman right at his heels.

"Here's company, Jack," said the gunman. "Found him skulkin' around outside. If you ask me, he saw plenty."

There were two more men in the room. One was stocky and bearded with bloodshot eyes, thick lips and no expression on his face. It was the second man who attracted all of Reed's attention.

He had studied enough reward posters of the outlaw to recognize Jack Braley when he saw him. Slender and of medium height, Braley was a mild-looking individual, smooth-skinned and perpetually smiling. An old knife scar at the right-hand corner of his mouth lifted his upper lip, leaving it on the thin tether of a smile.

He was wearing plain black pants tucked into worn half-boots. His shirt was a gaudy orange and a brilliant green neckerchief circled his throat. His eyes were blue and bland and almost kindly when viewed from a distance. But beneath their cool, unruffled surface flamed a cruel and speculative cunning. Reed knew at once that he was looking at a cold-blooded, iron-nerved killer.

Now Braley hauled his slender length out of a chair and came around the rough-hewn table. The cabin was disordered. The only furniture consisted of four sets of double-tiered bunks built into the wall, several packing boxes, two rickety chairs and the table.

"I reckon you're Jim Reed," said Braley. His eyes regarded Reed with a probing intensity. "The gent who braced Gulistan and Ormand."

Reed's expression did not change. Only his eyes flickered.

"News travels fast even out here," he observed.

"We have ways of gettin' information," Braley told him.

"Such as workin' under cover with Wright or Gulistan or Esmond?"

The bluntness of the question shook up the renegade. His arms lifted and Reed noticed that his fists were balled. Braley kept on smiling, but his eyes had turned to splinters of dark blue ice.

"Try again, Reed," he taunted slowly. "I don't fall for that trap. For all you'll ever know, we're workin' on our own."

"Sure." Reed looked squarely at him, his shoulders solid and muscular beneath his tight shirt. "We'll let that go. Nice business you have here. Good hideout. What's the price of rustled beef?"

The false smile lingered on Braley's face. With a leisurely gesture he drew his gun and checked the bullet loads.

"I wouldn't know," he said idly. Then his manner grew pensive. "I'm tryin' to figure how much I could get for you on the hoof."

"You goin' to do the job here?" asked the outlaw behind Reed.

A slow flush mounted through Reed's craggy features. There wasn't any inflection in the gunman's question. He might have been talking about the weather—but he wasn't. And Reed knew as well as he had ever known anything in his life that he was living on borrowed time.

He looked at Braley's smooth, smiling face. Something in the brutal amusement glittering there left Reed with a hollow sensation in the pit of his stomach. There was no mercy for him here. He had blundered into a trap. He had seen too much. His next ride would be at the end of a bullet.

All three outlaws watched him with a naked hunger shining out of their eyes. The sound of their aroused breathing tugged at Reed's nerves like a nagging, insistent hand, and his lips made a dry wedge against the growing bleakness of his face.

"How would you like it?" Braley inquired gently, twirling the gun in his fist. He looked soft and his voice was soft, but there was no softness in him. "In the belly or in the back?"

"Either way, Braley."

Reed's self-control was a hard and terrible thing to witness. His tanned, weather-beaten skin stretched more tightly across his high cheekbones as wildness began to crowd him.

Now, because they showed him no mercy, that virtue washed out of him and it left him with only his tough and unyielding will and a wicked violence that surpassed their own.

Braley's gun came up slowly, rising level with Reed's chest. Reed reached the end of his patience. He took two retreating steps until his shoulder blades touched the wall.

"You understand there's nothing personal in this," murmured Braley. "It's just that you stuck your nose into business that didn't concern you. That's never a safe thing to do."

"Don't apologize, Braley," said Reed through thin lips. "You have your work to do—and I have mine."

Then Reed's straining muscles exploded him into action. One moment he was pressed solidly against the wall, waiting for the bite of lead in his chest. The next he had braced himself there, his right boot arching upward. The tip of the boot struck Braley's weapon, knocked it from his fingers.

The gun fell with a dull clatter to the floor. Reed followed that kick with a lunge of his body. He drove a knee into the pit of Braley's belly, hit him with the bunched knuckles of his right hand, then flung himself on the floor.

The outlaw behind Reed yelled. His gun bucked against his wrist and a bullet slashed across the slack in Reed's shirt. He struck the floor on hands and knees. His fingers knotted around Braley's weapon and he snapped a shot at the man who had captured him, winging the fellow's wrist.

The renegade howled in pain, dropped his gun and clutched at his injured wrist with his free hand. Blood began to trickle slowly through his fingers. The third outlaw shot again but missed as Reed left the boards and came up against Braley. Reed locked his left arm about Braley's throat, hauled him backward against his own chest.

"Isn't that gun gettin' kind of hot to hold?"

The remaining outlaw caught the significance of Reed's question. Cursing under his breath, he relinquished the gun. Afterward, Reed pushed Braley away from him. Reeling against the wall, Braley planted his boots far apart in a quick struggle to regain his balance. A burning hatred flared briefly in his eyes, but the smile never left his lips and the deceptive, disturbing softness never left his voice.

"I underestimated you," said Braley. "It's a mistake I seldom make. You're even tougher than I've heard."

"Where do we go from here?" demanded the wounded renegade.

"Back to Outpost," replied Reed. "I don't know how well Sheriff Collier is fixed for board and lodging in the jail, but I reckon he can fix you up with some kind of free accommodations. But first you gents are goin' to help me drive those steers back where they belong."

Braley's lips curled derisively.

"That's a big order, friend. How do you know we'll help?"

Reed's features remained somber and taciturn. The only thing that moved in his face was a small muscle at the base of his jaw. He looked from the gun in his hand back to Braley.

"You've won this hand," admitted Braley, his manner languid and careless. "Better not crowd your luck."

"It's my luck and I'm the man to crowd it."

"Go ahead." Braley shrugged idly. "Don't forget you're all alone and you're buckin' somethin' that's bigger than any one man. Take my advice and clear out while you've got your hide."

"Keep your advice," said Reed and changed the subject. "If you prove a good swing rider I may be able to get you a southern exposure in the Outpost jail. Move outside into the yard now."

Braley's composure dropped from him and anger had its rough and surly way with his feelings. His two companions looked quizzically at him, then followed him to the yard.

"Rope your horses," Reed directed curtly. "Braley, when your pards have mounted, tie their ankles under their horses' bellies."

Braley grunted and stooped down to pick up the piggin' string Reed tossed to the ground at his feet.

"You enjoy yourself while you can," the outlaw grunted.

Reed told him: "I sure will."

With Reed's guns menacing him at every step Braley followed orders. When the two renegades were trussed to their saddles, Reed sauntered over to Braley and bound his ankles in a similar manner.

Swinging aboard the bay gelding, Reed let his hard voice hammer against all these men.

"Cut loose with your rope ends and chouse those steers toward the canyon. The cattle go to the Slash W. There they can be sorted and returned to their rightful owners. After that we'll visit Ben Collier."

Braley turned his horse toward the grazing steers. The other men circled and came up on the far side of the herd. In two or three minutes they had the beef on the move. Reed posted himself at drag.

Dust boiled up around the riders, and the ground shook under the rhythmic pounding of hoofs. Reed lifted his neckerchief up around his nose to protect himself from the billowing dirt. Braley and the others started riding ahead at a fast clip. Grimly Reed tilted his gun and placed a shot carefully over Braley's head. The outlaw pulled in his mount. He twisted about in the hull, his eyes bland and questioning.

"The next one will come closer," Reed warned tonelessly. "See that you and your men don't get too far ahead."

Braley grinned, his shoulders shaking with a strange and silent mirth. He was an odd character, seemingly passionless, always smiling, yet definitely dangerous.

8

THE valley narrowed abruptly as rocky ramparts closed in upon cattle and horses and men. Purple shadows slid up and down the towering granite walls. Reed pushed the stragglers along, never letting Braley or his companions shove too far ahead of him. And all the while he rode he was thinking of what he had found in the hidden valley and realizing that he was not much nearer a solution of his problem than he had been.

He was certain of only one thing. Braley and his gang were responsible for the actual rustling. Also, Braley was undoubtedly working with someone in the valley. But who that man might be Reed was unable to determine.

Reed had found cattle from all the neighboring spreads in the outlaw hideout, including those of Gulistan and Wright. It was, therefore, impossible to tell which rancher was double-crossing his friends—if the renegade leader really was one of the cowmen—for he had apparently been clever enough to steal some of his own beef to direct suspicion away from himself.

Of course, Ormand and Esmond were also suspects, particularly the latter. Holding mortgage notes on most of the outfits, Esmond was in a unique position to profit by a range war or by large-scale rustling against the cattlemen. If the big outfits lost enough beef they'd be compelled to default on their mortgage payments and the bank could foreclose. Yes, Clark Esmond would be in an enviable position to hasten the ruin of the cattlemen and insure defaulting on mortgage notes if he were directing the rustling activities. And the raids on the stages might be a concession on Esmond's part to let high-living outlaws secure huge amounts of cash which he was reluctant to pay out of his own pocket.

Cattle and riders came abruptly now to the end of the short, high-walled defile. The bawling critters were pushed into the thick tangle of brush that screened off the hidden gorge from the canyon on the other side of the valley. Bursting through the chaparral at a lumbering run, the steers were hazed down-canyon toward the foothills.

The drive continued through the growing

heat of early afternoon and the dust grew steadily thicker. It boiled up in great gray-brown clouds. Reed's throat became parched and dry and fatigue was a persistent drag on his stamina.

Gradually the twisting ravines and rocky precipices gave way before the gentle march of rolling hills. They left the badlands behind them and an hour and a half later threw the beef onto Slash W range.

They were descending a long grade with the scattered out-buildings of Wright's ranch a dim white blur in the distance when a rider cut out of the brush and quartered across the path of the on-rushing herd. Reed immediately kicked his mount into a run and pushed up along the right flank, noticing that the rider was Diana Wright.

She had her pinto going at a full gallop. Her sleek, dark hair streamed out beneath a fawn-gray sombrero and she came on steadily. Reed called out a warning, but his voice was lost in the thunder of hoofs.

Reed slammed his bay past Braley. He had seen Diana's saddle shift and slide sidewise. She lost her balance, made a frantic attempt to keep her seat. But the saddle kept slipping. She sawed on the reins, managed to slow the horse, but she could not prevent herself from pitching into space.

Diana landed on her hands and knees in the dust. She saw the steers converging on her and struggled up. She lurched forward a few feet, then tripped and fell again.

His heart contracting with a hollow dread, Reed lashed the bay on. He pounded past the longhorn leaders, swung in sharply toward the girl. He was almost on top of Diana when he hauled back on the reins, bringing the bay to a skidding halt.

Before the animal had completed its slide, Reed was out of the saddle. He struck the ground with bent knees, stumbled forward, recovered and reached for Diana. She was fighting to rise again. He scooped her up in his arms and rushed back to the fidgeting bay.

A great pall of dust spiraled close to them and the thunder of hoofs was a terrific din in their ears. It set up a heavy roaring in Reed's head. There was no turning the spooked cattle at this moment. They had scented a Slash W waterhole and were racing toward it. He could see their wild, staring eyes, their bobbing horns and knew how close and hard this thing would be.

Reed lifted Diana roughly into the saddle. Then, with the bay already leaping out in a fast run, he vaulted up behind her. The milling herd closed in around them. Reed found himself looking out upon a turgid sea of dappled, heaving bodies and ominously clacking horns.

One misstep now and he and Diana would be plunged into that boiling tide of thirst-maddened beef. But the bay kept on gamely, holding its own. Under Reed's careful guidance the horse veered gradually to the right until they hit the edges of the herd.

Another moment and the bay had won clear. The cattle rushed past, stirring up a great racket. Pulling in the bay, Reed let his glance swing around and noticed with a surge of exasperation that his captives had fled.

He saw Braley's two hirclings disappearing in a stand of trees, racing back toward the badlands. There was no sign of Braley. Angry and irritated because the renegades had slipped through his fingers while he was saving Diana, Reed looked down at her and made no attempt to hide his outraged feelings.

Diana twisted around and Reed saw that her face was streaked with dust. The palm of her left hand was lacerated and bleeding slightly, and the strain of her narrow escape from death had turned her pallid and completely breathless.

Reed eased himself out of the saddle. He held up his arms and lifted her down to the ground. For a brief moment her lithe, warm body was against him and he felt the bold strike of her dark eyes. She made no move to step away. There was a subtle, provocative invitation shining in her face. It was very real and very disturbing.

Diana wanted him to have his close and thorough look at her. There was something in her manner that told him she knew how much her nearness could stir a man. And so she waited this brief moment for the turbulent pull of Reed's impulses to shock his face into harsher lines. Reed watched her without a smile, holding himself straight and still, and when his expression failed to change, her hands came up behind his head. Impulsively she pulled his face down to hers and kissed him.

There was a hard, passionate flavor to that caress. Her lips were warm and demanding beneath his own, but now, for some unaccountable reason, it seemed to Reed that it was the straight-shouldered figure of Sally Drennan in his arms instead of Diana Wright.

He was suddenly recalling Sally's tanned face with the defiant thrust of her small chin; he was seeing how the tumult of rage enhanced her loveliness; and he was seeing the haunting loneliness in her eyes—a loneliness that matched the emptiness of his own existence.

Now, because he found no pleasure in kissing Diana, he pushed her almost roughly away. Her arms slid down from his neck and she gave him an odd, probing stare.

"That was a strange thing," Reed said, unable to control the unsteadiness in his speech.

Color crept up into Diana's fully rounded cheeks.

"I don't understand," she told him.

"My apologies to you," he murmured. He was awkward and ill at ease. "I had no right to do that."

"You mean you're sorry you kissed me?" Incredulity was in her face and her voice.

"As I see it," he said with difficulty, "you were upset by your narrow escape and feeling grateful."

"Grateful?" Diana repeated. Her eyes burned

with a fierce and angry intensity. "Did it ever occur to you that I might have wanted to kiss you and that saving my life had nothing to do with it?"

Reed managed a strained, twisted smile, but the soberness returned immediately to his cheeks.

"In my life I have known few women," he told her. "Perhaps that has been to my disadvantage. In any event, it has always been in my mind that when a man kisses a woman, he does so because his intentions are serious; because he regards her as his woman and she accepts him as her man."

Diana's cheeks whitened and that pallor deepened, by contrast, the rich, red line of her mouth. She stepped nearer suddenly enjoying the uneasy storm behind his slate-gray eyes.

"You're a strange man, Jim," she said and now her eyes were mocking and inviting him. "Your belief leaves no room for the man and woman who are attracted to each other at first sight and who answer the call of their own nearness because they recognize it as a force bigger than themselves and not to be ignored." She stopped and put her hands on his chest. "Oh, Jim, why are we talking here when—?"

Her words broke off while she lifted her face to his, and she remained still and unresisting, waiting for whatever he would do. Her thoughts ran warm and intimate, plucking at Reed with an insistent feminine attention. But now Reed braced himself and his hands came up to grasp her arms and pull them gently away.

"Not again, Diana," he said huskily.

A quiver ran through Diana's body. She had the stricken, unrelenting look of a woman who has just been struck by a man and is shocked and bewildered and angry all at once.

She had always been a strong-willed, stubborn girl and now her quick temper shone darkly through her skin. She lunged at Reed and the palm of her hand struck his right cheek a stinging blow.

"It isn't every man that has an opportunity to kiss me, Jim Reed," she said her, voice hot and wrathful. "I won't forget this and neither will you. If you remain alive in this valley you'll see the time when you'll come begging to kiss me."

Reed's eyebrows lifted, but his voice remained level and even.

"You are quite sure of yourself. I am sorry for it."

"Keep away from her, Reed!" shouted a new voice from a distance.

Diana and Reed pivoted, their attention jumping to the chaparral halfway up the slope behind them. Noel Hockett, the Slash W foreman, his face ravaged by quick fury, spurred his horse out of the bush.

"Diana," Hockett growled savagely as he skidded his big Morgan to a halt in front of them and jumped to the ground. "I saw you slap this man. If he laid a hand on you I'll break him in two."

Hockett's features were dark and belligerent. His shoulders were bowed and the ugly fires of jealousy flared in his slitted eyes.

"Start breakin', friend," Reed told him stonily. "What happened does not concern you."

Hockett swore and paced forward. Diana threw herself against him, grasping at his heavy arms, straining to hold him back.

"Don't, Noel. Not now!"

The ramrod shoved the girl roughly aside and his talk lashed out at Reed, guttural and savage.

"It's plenty of my business, Reed. I happen to be engaged to Diana, and I'll see that every man keeps his distance."

Surprise showed briefly in Reed's face. His eyes came around to Diana and he saw no denial in her angry glance. Slowly, then, a gray displeasure worried the corners of his long lips. A curt answer was on the tip of his tongue. But it was never uttered for five horsemen appeared on the ridge behind them and came thundering down the grade. They rode at a full gallop and Reed saw that Harry Wright, big and solid in his high-forked saddle, was in the lead. Directly behind him and flanked by three Slash W punchers rode Jack Braley.

A thin feeling of satisfaction oiled Reed's nerves. Some ironical turn of fate had sent Braley fleeing into Wright's hands. Part of the crew must have been hunting in the badlands for the missing cattle. Thus the one avenue of escape to Braley had proved his undoing. However, his two companions, striking out in a more northerly direction had managed to hit a thick belt of timber without encountering the Slash W horsemen.

"Reed, you're just the man I want to see," Wright greeted him as the five riders drew to a halt.

The rancher looked at Hockett and Diana, seeing the angry color in their cheeks. Afterward his glance went beyond them to the distant Slash W buildings where the glitter of the waterhole was blotted out by a cloud of dust and the milling forms of thirsty cattle.

"What's happened here?" Wright demanded, hard suspicion in his gray eyes. "The grass is all churned up and there's dust in the air. What are those cattle doing in my basin, Reed? I reckon you know the answer."

"Sure I do, but Braley knows more. Don't you, Jack?"

Hockett shoved forward, and there was an odd, unfathomable light in his narrowed eyes.

"By God, it is Jack Braley," he said. "I recognize him now. I've seen his picture on reward dodgers in town."

There was a casual, half insolent smile on the outlaw's face.

"Your luck, Reed, that I ran the wrong way."

"We caught this jasper rattlin' his hocks toward the badlands," murmured Harry Wright. "He was travelin' too fast to be out just for the ride and when we saw his legs tied under the saddle, we closed in on him. Then I saw it was Braley—recognized him from reward dodgers I've seen in town."

"Nice job you did savin' the girl from that beef," Braley told Reed. There was no animosity in his tone. He seemed friendly and quite content, yet Reed was aware that underneath that cool exterior the outlaw was a ruthless man and utterly without sentiment. "It wouldn't have been me, my friend. But that's where you'll slip some day. You're plenty tough, but that soft spot in you will ruin you."

Wright was puzzled and suspicious and for the moment found nothing to say.

"A favor for a favor," Reed suggested tersely. "Your cattle for Braley." He gestured toward the distant ranch buildings. "You'll find some of your own beef there along with some steers belonging to Gulistan and others of your neighbors. I rode over to the badlands this morning, ran into Braley and his friends and convinced them that it might be a good idea to return the stolen longhorns. Braley's your rustler. I have an idea there was a lot more beef up in the badlands two or three days ago, but they've gone across the state line."

"You tryin' to tell me you captured Braley yourself?" Wright asked, his tone disbelieving.

"Yeah, and two of his men. They helped me haze the beef down here—not without

106

some persuasion. They broke away when your daughter rode in front of the herd and her cinch broke, spilling her to the ground. It was her or the outlaws. Naturally, it had to be the girl."

"Where did you find the beef?" Wright demanded of Reed. "And who's payin' him to rustle Outpost cattle?"

"I don't know," said Reed. "Maybe it's you. It occurs to me you may have some legitimate cowhands workin' for you and with Braley poppin' right into your hands and with your crew recognizin' him, there was nothin' else to do but to dab your loop on him, even though his own gang is handlin' your dirty work."

Braley laughed, his smooth swarthy features tough and goading under the malicious humor.

"You've made similar accusations once before," Wright glared angrily. "I don't want to hear them again. I've got only one crew workin' my spread and they're real cowhands. If I knew who imported Braley to rustle the ranchers in Outpost blind, I'd go gunnin' for him right now."

Wright paused. His eyes were surly and truculent, but he made a tremendous effort to control his rage.

"I spoke to Sheriff Collier this mornin'," he

said more calmly. "It seems you told a straight story about Stacey. I am sorry about that. But if he tried to kill you, he had no orders from me."

Reed stood immobile at the head of the bay gelding. He hadn't yet made up his mind about Harry Wright and his cool skepticism showed on his cheeks. But all he said was:

"Some day I'll find the man who gave Stacey his orders. When I do I'll talk to him in gunsmoke."

Hockett moved past Braley and swung to face the Slash W owner.

"We'd better get Braley to town and have him locked up in jail," he said, an odd urgency in his voice. "Want me to handle it?"

"You're too anxious for the job," interrupted Reed flatly. "Maybe you're a friend of Braley's so I'd better handle it myself."

Black fury climbed through the ramrod. His features turned livid and challenging."

"Are you hinting I'd let him go?"

Reed shrugged his shoulders in an idle gesture.

"I trust no man for that job but myself. Wright pays you foreman's wages, but until I'm sure where your loyalties lay as well as the loyalties of every other man on the Outpost range, I'll play this my way."

Hockett cursed and his wide, stocky frame bowed in a crouch. Rashness was pinching his muscles, turning him wild and desperate. Wright saw the danger signals in his eyes and flung out a restraining hand.

"Hold off, Hockett!" Wright whirled to Reed. "Man, you seem to take pleasure in provokin' trouble. You talk fight at every turn. In this valley it won't get you a long life."

"I'll live long enough to take company along when I go out," Reed murmured flatly, the stubbornness of his will showing through his brittle speech. "My experience here compels me to trust no man. There was Johnny Drennan, a Gulistan hand—but an outlaw. And there was Stacey, your own hand, who tried to kill me. How do you know you can trust Hockett or others on your outfit?"

"How dare you say that?"

It was Diana speaking. Turning his gaze upon her, Reed saw the flaming color in her cheeks, the bitter curve of her mouth. He had wounded her pride, and her loyalty to her father and his crew now became a fierce, unyielding thing.

109

"I'd trust any man in this valley before I'd trust you," she added hotly.

Hockett was pleased. His eyes slid around to the girl, hungry and demanding and she gave him a brief, bright smile.

"Keep out of this, Diana," snapped Wright. He turned to one of his crew. "Anderson, you ride back to the ranch with Diana."

The girl was about to protest, but something in her father's rough glance made her turn away and limp to her horse. Hockett gave her a lift into the saddle. Then she picked up the reins, swung her pinto about and jogged down the grade beside the Slash W puncher.

"You speak of trustin' no one," Wright said after a moment. "I can say the same about you. You're a stranger in Outpost. You bring death on your arrival. Two men try to kill you and you cash their chips. You're offered two jobs, yet you take neither. You play a lone hand and you meddle in things that don't concern you. Or do they? It still occurs to me that you might be a federal marshal."

There was a dark and intense reserve on Reed's angular face. His eyes never ceased to watch Wright or his crew.

"You see a badge on me?" he inquired.

"No. You might be carryin' it in your boot."

"Sure, but don't let it worry you. Now about those cattle. Cut out those with your brand and leave the rest to be picked up by whoever they belong to."

"Not so fast," protested Wright. "I'd like to know where you found those cattle and what your stake in this business is."

"You keep guessin' about my stake for a spell," Reed told him curtly. "As for the cattle it'd be kind of hard to describe whereabouts in the badlands Braley has his hideout. I'd have to lead you there. There's time for that later. Right now I'm headin' for town with Braley. In the meantime, put double guards on your beef. Braley's crew of gunmen is still roamin' the hills."

"All right, Reed," said Braley, speaking before Wright could answer Reed. "Let's move on."

"Kind of impatient to get to jail, aren't you?" Wright asked.

"Yeah, I could use some sleep and I figure the Outpost jail ought to be fixed up with some nice soft beds."

Braley grinned at Wright, then let his eyes

111

drift to Hockett while the sly amusement around his mouth steadily increased.

Reed stepped to his horse and mounted, afterward lifting his hand to Wright and riding off beside the renegade. They cut south, angling for the stage road that wound through the lower hills.

9

LONG shadows of twilight were darkening the ruby and granite cliffs of the badlands far behind them when Reed and Braley jogged into Outpost's single main street. Men lounging along the walks watched them curiously. They passed the hotel and a man seated on a chair that had been tipped back against the wall, suddenly jounced the chair down on its front legs and hauled himself to his feet. His voice carried in a piercing wave across the street's narrow boundary.

"Hell, that Reed hombre has Jack Braley, the outlaw!"

The man came off the hotel veranda and pegged along the walk. He rushed into the saloon and came out in half a minute. Other men barged through the batwings after him and a mob began to form, moving in a phalanx after the two horsemen.

"Nothin' like a little entertainment for the town," said Braley, gesturing over his shoulder.

113

"Your fame travels with you," Reed replied dryly.

The clamor along the street mounted steadily and Reed set the horses moving more rapidly. They angled in toward the hitch rack in front of the jail and Reed dismounted. He took out his knife and cut the thongs which bound Braley's ankles, then signaled him to get down.

Drawing his gun, Reed pushed Braley up the steps leading to the sheriff's office. The door was half open, a trickle of yellow lamplight flushing out into the dim twilight of the street. Braley stepped inside and Reed was close on his heels, kicking the door shut to close out the curious throng.

Collier, half-asleep in his swivel chair, his booted feet crossed on top of his battered desk, swung his legs to the floor and bounded up. His tobacco-stained, handlebar mustache quivered in surprise and his eyes were bleary with shock.

"Hello, Collier," said Reed. "Have you got room to put up Jack Braley for a spell?"

Collier did not immediately answer. His blocky shoulders beneath his cowhide vest stirred restlessly and his mouth hung open.

"Where did you find him?" he asked faintly.

"In the badlands with a lot of stolen Outpost beef."

Braley laughed softly and Collier squinted queerly at him.

"What's so funny?" Collier inquired irritably.

"Do you believe Reed?" Braley asked. He slanted a glance at Reed and his eyes were sharp and wise and mocking.

Sudden doubt crept into Collier's face. He gazed toward the street, heard the hard run of the crowd's talk. Abruptly he strode to the windows and drew the blind. Then he came back to Reed and his hand slid to the butt of his Colt and stayed there.

"Maybe you'd better explain," he suggested.

"Sure, I'll write you a letter," snapped Reed tartly. "This is the man who's been leading the rustlin' gang. I figure somebody else is behind him. Somebody in this town. What happened to Drennan and Stacey convinces me of that. The man might be Gulistan or Wright or Esmond or even Val Ormand. I don't know."

Braley's continued mocking amusement seemed to shake Collier, add fuel to the fires of skepticism seething in his mind. Reed ignored that silent laughter and related all that had happened during the day, giving only a meager description of where the cattle had been found.

"That's the story," he concluded gruffly, "and here's the man you want. The next step is to find his boss. When you do, you'll smash the trouble in Outpost."

"You tellin' me how to run my office?" Collier demanded.

"I'm tellin' you what looks to be fairly obvious. I've an idea he might even know about that attempted stage hold-up yesterday."

Collier scowled, his face turning cold and dark with disapproval. It was a stiff blow to his pride that another man should bring in the outlaw who had been sought for many weeks by an entire county. Besides, like other people in this trouble-torn town, there was no trust in Collier.

"What are you figurin' on gettin' out of this?" he asked.

"Nothin', Collier, except to see that justice is done."

Collier snorted. His lips rolled together in a dissenting line.

"I've got you tabbed now. You're a bounty hunter," he sneered. "There's a thousand

116

dollars' reward on Braley's head. You aim to collect that money?"

"Guess again."

"Why guess?" snapped Braley. He waited for Collier to glance toward him before his expression changed and rage warped his features. "Doesn't it seem odd, Sherriff, that one man should be able to bring in an outlaw several posses couldn't capture, and that a total stranger in unfamiliar country should find that outlaw without any difficulty?"

"Yeah, it does," agreed Collier. To Reed he said: "I've still got my doubts about you."

"Go on havin' them, Collier. And now, if you don't throw Braley in a cell, I'll do it myself. As for trailing Braley, I'll admit I had to have luck to run him down."

"You lie!" raged Braley. The sudden change in the renegade's manner pulled Reed fully around. Braley was trembling in fury, yet behind his apparent wrath Reed thought he detected the old sly amusement. He knew, then, that this was an act. But Collier did not know it and would be affected by it.

"What do you mean?" Collier asked.

Slowly the sheriff leaned down to turn up the wick of the lamp. The brighter illumination showed the tautness in his blocky shape, the deep crease in the flesh between his eyes.

"I mean," said Braley savagely, "that Reed is a member of my own wild bunch. How else would he find me? He's been hankerin' to get control of the gang for weeks and I've had to watch him closely. This morning I was careless and he got the drop on me. He brought me to town after the rest of my bunch had ridden off from our camp. He was plannin' to collect the bounty on my head, then be in the clear to ramrod the boys."

With a bellow of rage Braley whirled and leaped at Reed, butting him with his head and driving him back against the door. A blinding light danced in Reed's eyes for a moment, and his teeth snapped together with an audible click. Then he lifted his left arm in a short, wicked arc, his knuckles catching Braley on the point of the chin and slamming him against the sheriff. Their legs got entangled and both men toppled to the floor.

"Nice actin', Braley," said Reed, rubbing his dully aching jaw. His teeth felt as if they had been driven up into his gums.

Braley rose. He showed Reed a brief flash of his sly humor, the veil dropped over his features and when Collier looked at him he was more furious than he had ever been.

"It's no act," he fumed. "You've double-crossed me and I'll kill you if I ever get a chance. If Collier had any sense he'd realize—"

"I'm beginnin' to see it," said Collier grimly, pulling himself to his feet. "You're a queer number, Reed. First I figured you for a gunhawk, then a marshal and just now a bounty hunter. But I reckon you're one of Braley's wild bunch so I'll lock you both up."

"Don't try it," Reed warned flatly. There was a tough, restless curl to his lips. "And keep your hand away from your gun. I want no fight with you, but at the same time I do not intend to be crowded."

Collier stood beside his desk, his blocky figure slightly crouched, his right arm tense and uneasy above his gun. But the longer he waited, the longer he watched the hard toughness so real and plain to see in Reed's features, the heavier grew the weight of uncertainty in him.

"I could call for help and in two minutes you'd be finished," Collier said lamely.

"Try it and see what happens."

"Don't let him bluff you!" said Braley.

"I'm still waiting," said Reed implacably.

119

"All right. All right."

Collier's words might have meant anything and Reed was resolved to have all the issues clear and sharp.

"Lock Braley up now and don't worry about that bounty money. I'm not intersted in it. And if you're lookin' for me at any time, I'll be around."

A long, weary breath spilled from Collier's lungs. Slowly he turned to the half-open drawer of his desk and removed a ring of keys. He gestured to Braley to precede him down the corridor that led to the cell-block in the rear of the building.

"So long, Reed," said Braley as the cell door clanged shut upon the outlaw. For once the smile was missing from his face and his eyes were entirely unreadable. "You hold acres right now. Who knows, maybe the next hand you'll be dealt deuces."

Reed made no comment and walked outside, and the small crowd still lingering by the hitch rack broke to let him through.

Going to the weary bay, he mounted and jogged down to the livery stable and left the animal there. Dusk had deepened into full darkness now and up and down the street lamplight began to make its creamy yellow glitter. The westbound stage rolled in with a harsh clatter of sound, high wheels skidding in the dust as the driver kicked on the brake. A half dozen riders from one of the outlying ranches galloped in and put up at one of the hitch rails, afterward bowlegging their way past the swinging doors of the Second Chance Saloon.

Reed lingered in the dark well of the livery stable entrance, watching the town come to life around him. Men sauntered by, gave him their keen and careful scrutiny, then turned away when they found that attention returned with a bold intensity.

Exploring his cartridge belt with nimble fingers, Reed saw that several loops were empty. Although he was hungry after his day-long ride, he delayed eating and moved toward the Mercantile.

The odor of coffee and flour and aging leather assailed his nostrils when he entered the store. He glanced toward one side of the interior, his eyes lingering on several hand-tooled leather saddles and bridles. Then he sauntered over to the scarred counter behind which were stacked beans and flour, bolts of cloth and guns and ammunition.

Lance Koenig shuffled out from the back room, rubbing the palms of his hands together.

"What will it be?" Koenig inquired.

"A box of .45 shells."

Koenig's pale eyes traveled to the empty loops of Reed's cartridge belt.

"You been hunting?"

"Yeah."

"Antelope or men?"

"Men." Reed's tone was curt. He was not in the mood for idle talk. "You gettin' those bullets?"

Koenig moved to the shelf at his back and reached toward the stacked boxes of shells. His back was still turned to Reed when he asked: "Heard some excitement down the street. What was it?"

"Jack Braley, the outlaw, was just brought in," Reed told him.

Koenig came around swiftly. He gave Reed a sharp look.

"Who got him? Not Collier, I reckon."

"No, it wasn't Collier. It was me."

Koenig smiled. His good-natured countenance took on a beaming lightness. He leaned across the counter.

"I don't know what brought you to Outpost, Reed, but you sure do get around."

"Yeah?"

Reed left that one word hanging in the air, taut and challenging.

"I watched you last night. You can take care of yourself and I've a feeling that when trouble breaks you'll be on the right side."

Reed remained wary. He wasn't sure if Koenig was just being talkative or if he were just fishing for information.

"Everybody in this town seems to be worried about what side I'm on. Which would you say was the right side?"

Koenig shrugged and waited till Reed examined the box of shells. Breaking open his Colt, Reed inserted fresh loads in the empty chambers, then filled his cartridge loops from the box. He paid Koenig and was starting away from the counter when the storekeeper spoke again.

"Catching Braley must have kept you busy," said the Mercantile owner. "I guess you didn't hear the latest news."

"What news?" he demanded.

"The town council gave Sally Drennan her

123

notice this mornin'. They're callin' in another school teacher."

A dark scowl spread across Reed's bruised, craggy features.

"On account of her brother?"

Koenig nodded, a hint of sadness in his pale cheeks.

"They figured they can't trust the teachin' of the town's children to the daughter and sister of outlaws."

"This is a hell of a town," Reed said, and anger pulled strongly at his lip corners. "Is a woman to blame for the mistakes of her family?"

"It's goin' to be tough on her," Koenig admitted. "As for Johnny, he never had much of a chance to go straight. Everybody hounded him, said bad blood would tell—that he had his father's wild, owlhoot streak in him. Sure, he was wild and reckless, but not bad—at least, not until they made him so by freezin' him out of any decent job on the range. I reckon the council wouldn't have kept Sally in the school if they could have gotten someone else."

Reed was conscious of a dull, inner pressure. He would always remember the fierce, bright courage in Sally's eyes when she had defied the mass enmity of an entire town.

"Who is on the council?" he asked.

"Wright, Ormand and Esmond. They gave Sally her notice right after Johnny was buried."

Koenig's announcement produced an unruly disturbance in Reed. By killing Sally's brother he became indirectly responsible for this fresh misfortune in the girl's life.

"Where will she go?" Reed demanded.

"Your guess is as good as mine," Koenig replied sadly. "She has no relatives, no friends here. I am surprised at your interest."

"I cannot forget that I am partly to blame for her trouble."

Reed paced to the front door, stared moodily out into the street, then came back again.

"You do much business in your store?" he inquired.

"Some. Why?"

"Enough to take on help?"

Surprise put slack lines across Koenig's cheekbones.

"You lookin' for work?" he queried.

"I'm thinkin' of Sally Drennan," Reed said. "Maybe you could give her a job, waitin' on customers."

125

"I'd like to, but my business isn't good enough for that. What little I could afford to pay her wouldn't amount of much."

Reed's glance was riveted intently upon the storekeeper.

"You worried about people takin' their trade elsewhere?"

"Not at all." There was swift denial in Koenig's tone. "I've known Sally since she was a toddler. Nothin' I wouldn't do for her— if I could. Wait!" Koenig's face brightened. "Maybe Ed Purcell at the hotel could use another waitress. I'll speak to him about it."

"Do that," snapped Reed quickly. "Tell him to send word to the girl that he can use her in the hotel dining room. I don't give a damn if he needs a waitress or not. If he hires her I'll take care of the salary myself. But don't ever tell her I had anythin' to do with it."

An odd, misty light came into Koenig's eyes. He looked closely at Reed, seeing the unyielding toughness of the man, the turbulent run of his feelings, yet also seeing a softness beneath that hard exterior which others seldom noticed. It tempered Koenig's judgment of Reed, impelled him to stretch his hand across the counter.

"It is a fine thing you wish to do," he said. Their hands met in a brief, firm clasp. "I shall make it my business to see Purcell tonight. I think he will agree." The storekeeper paused, searching scrupulously in his mind for further words. "If you ever need a friend call on me."

Reed fumbled with a concealed pouch in the inner side of his cartridge belt. He took out some bills and handed them to Koenig.

"I leave it to you or Purcell to name the salary. Use this. When it's gone come to me for more—if I'm still here by that time."

Koenig started to take the money, then pushed it back to Reed.

"I've been thinkin'," he said softly. "I'm an old man and all alone. You have opened my eyes to something I should have seen myself. I cannot take what little money I have saved with me. I will handle this matter of Sally's wages myself."

"As you wish," said Reed. But restlessness kept nagging at him and he was not yet content. "Where do I find her cabin?"

"Three miles north of the town the road forks," Koenig told him promptly. "Take the right-hand branch for a half mile. Her cabin is at the foot of a long grade. You can't miss it."

10

WITH impatience driving him, Reed turned out of the Mercantile and went to the livery to hire another horse. Afterward, he struck straight north along the stage road, ignoring the pointed glances of townsmen and punchers. He passed no riders along the road and when he hit the bottom of the hill beyond the trail fork he saw the bright flicker of lamplight punching a broad hole across the night's gloom. The dark bulk of a cabin gradually took shape around that increasing yellow brilliance.

He rode boldly up to the yard and dismounted. He was walking toward the cabin when the door was flung open and Sally came outside.

"Who is there?" she called.

"Jim Reed," he answered and moved nearer. He saw her body stiffen, saw the way her hand went out to grip the cabin wall at her side.

"Keep riding," she said tonelessly.

"I want only a moment."

128

"You are not welcome here."

Suddenly she darted inside the cabin. She reappeared at once. This time there was a rifle in her hands and the barrel lifted to center on Reed's chest.

"I have heard the news about your job," he said doggedly while his eyes kept watching the rifle and his stomach muscles were knotting. You could never tell what an angry, emotionally upset girl would do with a rifle. "I am sorry about that."

"Turn around and walk back to your horse," Sally ordered relentlessly, "or I'll shoot.'

There was a note of heartbreak in the girl's voice. She had been through something and whatever lightness and laughter had been in her was gone, leaving a hollow shell of despair.

The lamplight streaming from the room picked out golden glints in her hair, and her beauty, her womanliness, was more compelling than it had ever been. Reed was a lonesome man and his life had run in deep and perilous paths. He had never thought seriously of any woman. Yet, the nearness of this girl was a haunting pressure upon him. She upset him, made him unsure of himself.

"I do not blame you for what you think," he

129

said carefully. "I have said I was sorry about the things that have happened. Is there something I can do?"

"Yes," she murmured, her lips hardly moving. "Please go."

She had hardened herself against him and the solid thrust of her contempt was an unscalable barrier between them. She was a woman with the wildness of this land shining out of her clear and beautiful lines. But at this moment she showed Reed a side of her nature that was altogether cold and reserved.

He felt the sting of a lingering regret, knew that there was little he could do or say, yet somehow he couldn't bring himself to go.

"Shoot if you will," he murmured. "I will not lift my hand against you."

He took another step toward her. He saw her shoulders stir to the aroused surge of her emotions, and his nerves began to quiver with a tension he could not control. He was waiting for the sharp blast of the rifle, for she looked desperate enough to go to any lengths to have her own will in this matter.

Reed approached to within three feet of Sally. Each clock-tick of time was an eternity. She watched him grimly with the flame in her eyes

130

burning higher and higher. Then the rifle lowered and her shoulders lost their squareness.

"That is better," he said and waited a moment before asking: "What will you do now that you've lost your school?"

"What I will do is no concern of yours," she told him bluntly.

Reed stared beyond her, past the half-open door. He saw that the cabin was neat and orderly. There were two worn suitcases in the front room and several neatly tied packages.

"I think I have the answer," he murmured and made his voice deliberately goading. "I was mistaken in you. You are quittin'."

"I do as I please."

"Sure, and if you leave Outpost now you will be doing just what Esmond and the rest expect you to do."

Sally's outraged glance seared into Reed. The pride in her was like a bar of iron. He had struck at the weakest spot in her armor. Now she stepped toward him and pushed against his chest with her hands.

"Get out!" she cried. She flung her voice at him with the stinging impact of a whiplash. "It is my brother who is dead. And it was you who killed him—a man who lives by his guns."

Reed had hurt her as he had wanted to hurt her. Now for some reason he could not explain he felt impelled to break the vow of his secrecy. Always the lone-wolf, trusting no one but himself and not caring how others judged him, he now found himself concerned because this girl thought ill of him.

"You have called me a gunman," he mused, the black shadows of his past ridging his high-cheekboned face. "In a sense you are correct. I live by the power of my guns, but I have never killed a man without a justifiable reason for doing so—and only then when there was no other course open to me. You may be surprised to learn that I came to Outpost with a definite job to do and that I am a federal marshal."

"A marshal!" Sally repeated, shock springing her eyes wide.

"Yes, I am here to put an end to the trouble in this alley. It was my misfortune to meet your brother in that stagecoach. What happened then could not be avoided. You can believe that or not."

"If you are a lawman, show me your badge," Sally said stiffly.

"That I cannot do," he replied with a wry grimace. "I lost it on my arrival."

132

"Very convenient, I'd say."

"Convenient for the man who tried to have me killed last night. You may have heard about that. I figure that badge has been found. And the man who found it has a guilty conscience, guessed who it belonged to and tried to get me out of the way."

"I heard the story," she said. "Red Stacey tried and you killed him. That keeps your record perfect. One man a day."

Scorn put an icy quality in Sally's talk and she was fiercely glad when she saw that her remark penetrated the thick covering of his reserve. His face turned hard and implacable and his eyelids narrowed. A quick, angry retort fled to his lips, but he stifled it. He replaced his hat on his head and turned back to his horse, swinging up to the saddle without another word, and spurred out of the yard.

All during the ride to town Reed's thoughts remained dark and full of misery. Sally Drennan's hatred bothered him more than he cared to admit, and he was unable to thrust the haunting memory of her loveliness from his mind.

Leaving the horse at the livery, he went back to the hotel and ate a solitary supper. Afterward, feeling restless, he moved down to the Second Chance Saloon and had a couple of drinks at the bar before sitting down in a poker game.

He played for three hours, losing heavily at first, then recouping his losses with some judicious raising and clever bluffing. Yet, all the while he played, part of his mind centered upon the trouble that had brought him to Outpost.

There was a pressure in his shoulders that would not leave and the feeling of evil remained steadily with him. It was something he could not explain. But, because this premonition of trouble to come had never betrayed him in the past, he lingered at the table and each man who entered the saloon became the subject of his careful attention.

Near midnight when the saloon had begun to empty two men sauntered past the swinging doors. Reed's glance lifted casually to them, then he stiffened. One of the newcomers was the flat-faced individual who had been with Jack Braley in the hidden valley.

Both men glanced warily about the room and Reed lowered his head, pretending keen interest in his five cards. But inside him his blood was boiling and the warning of evil grew definitely stronger. It occurred to him that the Braley gang might be planning a jail-break, and these two hardcases had entered the saloon to make a hasty survey of their chances of being interrupted or thwarted.

They downed their whiskey at one gulp, flipped coins on the bar and sauntered outside again. Impatience drove Reed to his feet as he flung down his cards.

"I'm callin' it a night, gents," he said.

Cashing in his chips, he strode between the cluster of poker tables to the swinging doors. Outside he stepped into the veranda shadows, letting his gaze slide up and down the dark street.

The only light came from the hotel and several bar-rooms still catering to customers. Yonder, beyond the first intersection, the false-fronted stores and shacks were shrouded in gloom.

At first Reed saw no sign of the two men. Then he heard the rataplan of hoofs, noticed the bobbing shapes of two horsemen cantering out of town. He listened carefully and heard those traveling hoofbeats come to a halt farther on.

The feeling of things going wrong plucked at

him. He left the saloon porch and strode down the walk, keeping to the shadows that hugged the buildings. The street was deserted and became darker as he hurried past the hotel.

He went past the first intersection, then stopped close against the wall of the blacksmith shop to listen. There was no sound now, and the silence paced on, deadly and ominous. Then, as he was about to go forward a horse stamped its hoofs in the dust somewhere ahead of him.

Moving cautiously, he slid past three more frame structures until the one-story bank building thrust its white bulk against the surrounding darkness. He saw a drifting shape, that resolved itself into a horse and rider, leaving the hitch rail and vanish into an alley.

An electric feeling of frenzy hammered up and down Reed's spine and the old wildness got into his blood stream. He ducked into the first alley he reached, sped back to the rear street. He was sprinting past an abandoned feed barn when he heard the full, muted sound of an explosion. That muffled concussion sent him ahead with the fear that he was already too late.

He ran past three more darkened buildings

before the bulk of the bank appeared before him. He had a brief glimpse of four horses ground-tied near a grove of trees, of a man posted beside them. Then the echo of Reed's pounding boots jerked that man around and a gun barked twice in rapid succession.

Bullets droned past Reed, but none found a target. Then his own gun was coming out and he was swinging in toward the rear door of the bank. A white plume of smoke trailed out of the half-open door. A gunshot spanked the hollow stillness inside the bank, then three men spilled through the doors opening. Two of them carried sacks in their hands.

Reed laid his fire on the third man as the latter's gun swung toward him. He felt his Colt buck solidly against his wrist. A red tongue of flame hosed from the tilting muzzle and the man on the bank steps staggered drunkenly. Then that man's gun blazed furiously.

An explosion boxed Reed's ears. His head seemed to dissolve in a sea of pain. His eyes misted over and he struggled frantically to hang on to consciousness.

He fell to his hands and knees, bowed head lolling limply between his arms. With a tremendous effort of will he lifted up his smoking gun, but he couldn't find the strength to drop hammer on another shot. And so he plunged on his face and a wave of blackness engulfed him.

11

CONSCIOUSNESS returned slowly to Reed. With it came an immediate awareness of throbbing pain along the top of his skull. There was a gray fog in his brain and a strange lassitude in all his limbs.

He was lying on his face and the raw, pungent taste of dirt was in his mouth. He rolled over on his back, all his movements awkward and uncertain. It was while he was hooking his elbows beneath him for support that the angry murmur of voices reached him.

One hand lifted involuntarily to his scalp. He brought it away, feeling the stickiness of blood in his palm. The glare of a bull's-eye lantern shone on his face and he raised his eyes to stare at the ring of men around him.

In one tight group he saw Clark Esmond, Val Ormand and Brad Gulistan. Across from them stood Sheriff Collier, glowering down at him, his big gnarled hand wrapped firmly around the battered walnut stock of a Colt forty-five.

"So that bullet didn't kill you, after all?"

growled Clark Esmond. He held himself rigid and his broad jaws were working with an anger he made no attempt to control. "Before this night is over you'll wish it had."

For a brief moment all the figures in front of Reed swam dizzily. He shook his head to clear it. Strain piled up and a feeling of menace nagged harshly at him.

Deliberately he placed his palms in the dust behind him and used his arms as a fulcrum to lever himself to his feet. He stood there uncertainly in the back street behind the bank while his mind raced to recall all the details of this situation that should be remembered.

"Quit talkin' in riddles," he murmured. "The bank was robbed and—"

Sheriff Ben Collier came around to face him and he jabbed his gun muzzle into Reed's midriff.

"We know all about it," he interrupted tartly. His mustache quivered and his seamed features were dark and unsparing. "Fifty thousand dollars in coin and currency was taken. Jed Stuart, the cashier, who was workin' late on account of roundup time, was killed. Maybe it wasn't your gun that finished him.

"But before he died he said he thought he

winged one of the masked robbers with a lucky shot. I'm guessin' you're the one he hit and I'm arrestin' you for murder and robbery."

There was a growing clamor of sound among the spectators. Reed recognized the import of that undercurrent of talk and his jaw set grimly.

"No need for an arrest," said Esmond savagely, forgetting his dignity in the passion of this unguarded moment, "when we have so many trees handy."

The banker's words put verbal expression to the ugly thoughts and impulses that drove every man in the crowd.

"String him up!" someone yelled and the cry was repeated, quickly spreading from man to man. They surged nearer and the sheriff had to shove the closest men back. Collier's hands brushed against Brad Gulistan, but he swung clear. He signaled to someone behind Reed. Two men stepped up then and gripped Reed's arms.

"It's the only way to handle this," Gulistan flung at the crowd. "Hang Reed as an example to his friends that Outpost has had its fill of outlaws and gun-slingers."

All of Gulistan's swaggering confidence had returned. He was a big man; his voice fitted his bigness and he liked the strident sound of it. There was no tolerance in him and no pity and he wanted his own way in this matter.

But Gulistan's massiveness made no impression on Reed, for Reed was tough and hard in his own compelling way. He was thoroughly conscious of the thin tether of restraint that held the crowd away from violence.

Keeping himself stiff and alert, he stared at Gulistan with a bright heat showing in his eyes until the rancher had to drop his gaze.

"It seldom fails," he said. "A big man stirs up a big wind." He enjoyed the way temper leaped in Gulistan's face, the way killing impulses churned in his eyes. "My only part in this business was a futile attempt to stop the raiders from gettin' away."

He gave a terse explanation of all that had happened, bitterness and impatience edging his words when he noticed how his talk fell on disbelieving ears.

"Luck wasn't with me," he concluded doggedly. "One of the renegades fired and creased me with a slug. I wasn't inside that bank."

"That's a helluva story, Reed," sneered Val

Ormand, speaking for the first time. He was as dark and debonair as ever and his dislike for Reed was a very real thing. "You're not half as good a liar as you are a killer."

Rage built up its insidious torment within Jim Reed and he kept his burning glance upon Ormand. He felt the solid sweep of antagonism washing all around him and made one last plea to the crowd's logic.

"There's one point everyone seems to be overlookin'," he said. "And it's the fact that if I'd wanted to grab that bank money, my best chance was the day when I brought in the stage after the attempted raid. It doesn't make sense that I'd drive a coach full of money into town, then risk my life tryin' to steal it."

"I've wondered about that," murmured Collier, pushing in front of Val Ormand. There was an intentness, a heavy impact in the lawman's speech and manner that drew Reed's attention. "But there's no denyin' the mask we found inside your shirt or the thousand dollars in new bills stickin' in your pants pocket. A wanderin' gunhawk doesn't pack that kind of dinero in his jeans."

Eyes spring wide with shocked amazement, Reed watched Collier extend both wrinkled hands toward him. There was a black cloth mask in the left hand, and the fingers of the sheriff's right hand closely gripped a bunch of crisp new bills.

Reed scowled, his mind immediately recognizing the implications of this evidence.

"Whoever wants me out of the way has decided to do a thorough job," he murmured flatly. "That mask and the money with it was planted on me. Somebody in this town is afraid of me—afraid I know too much about the trouble in Outpost."

"Maybe you do know too much," said Clark Esmond quickly. "Maybe you could tell us who's the man behind you—if there is one."

The banker's broad cheeks were puffed out with importance and for this moment he was as domineering as Gulistan.

"Make him talk," a man yelled at the back of the crowd. "That's the only way we'll get to the bottom of things here."

But Reed lifted his voice above the aroused murmur of the mob.

"Ask yourself, Esmond. You might get a faster answer."

Esmond came forward. Before Collier could stop him he had swung a knuckled fist to Reed's mouth. Reed's head snapped back; his teeth clicked together and afterward a trickle of blood seeped from the corner of his mouth. Reed shook his head, stared straight at the banker and there was an unholy gleam in his gray eyes.

"What do you mean by that?" demanded Esmond.

"You're so damned busy accusin' me of murder on trumped-up evidence that it might be a cover-up. I wonder if anyone ever figured how easily a banker could make himself top dog in any cowtown by helpin' to rob his own bank, thus liquidating his own assets to have an excuse to freeze all money and foreclose on mortgages."

Esmond was swearing savagely before Reed finished and others in the crowd were getting impatient as the hanging mood still ruled them.

"Since you've come to Outpost you've brought nothin' but trouble and death," snapped Esmond. His heavy brows drew down like dark awnings over his eyes. "I heard about Braley's capture. It looks like Braley called the turn when he said you were doublecrossin' him."

Esmond paused dramatically, letting his hard, confident gaze drift over the crowd.

"More than Braley and more than the money that's been lost," he resumed slowly and distinctly, "I'm thinkin' of Jed Stuart's two kids. Jed's been bringin' them up since their mother died three years ago. He's been both a father and a mother to them. But now they're homeless and this man—Jim Reed, a stranger and a gunman—is the man who helped make those two youngsters orphans."

A stab of remorse struck Reed when he learned about Stuart's children. It would be tough on them, and he wished fervently that he had arrived on the scene earlier. Stuart's life might have been saved.

But it was too late. What was done was done. A man could have regrets, but they were never a help, never a solution.

"We're wastin' time here with palaver!" burst out Ormand. "The quicker we hang him the better off Outpost will be."

"I agree with Ormand on that," said the banker. He fumbled in an inside coat pocket. "Here, sheriff, is a list of serial numbers of the currency that was sent on the stage. I always have such a list prepared for an emergency like this. Suppose you check those bills you hold with some of the numbers on this sheet."

Collier, a little uneasy at the temper of the on-lookers, hesitated before accepting the paper from Esmond. His eyes scanned the list for several seconds before an exclamation burst from him.

"Every one of these bills tallies with a number on this sheet!"

"There's all the proof you need that Reed was in on that bank hold-up," said Esmond with a triumphant smile.

"Esmond," growled Gulistan. "I'll tell you to your face that I've got no use for you since you refused an extension of my mortgage note, but I'm sidin' you in this affair. Those bills are proof enough for me. I've got the rope. Let's get this job over with."

Someone in the crowd had passed him a rope. Now Gulistan's arm flicked upward and a noose twirled through the air to drop over Reed's head. But Reed was moving with the rope. A desperate lunge drove him clear of the men who had been holding him. Then, before Gulistan could snap the noose tight around his neck. Reed shot his hands upward, grabbed the rope and lifted it over his head.

Simultaneously Collier whirled around, drove

his shoulder against Gulistan, pushing him backward.

"Hold on!" Collier growled. His unruly gray hair formed a somber cowl above his dead-serious face. This was a dangerous moment for him. He didn't relish his position but he was forcing himself to do what duty called upon him to do. "There'll be no lynchin' while I'm sheriff of Outpost. Get that straight, all of you!"

"What do you want to do, Collier?" demanded Gulistan. He towered above the hollow-cheeked lawman and he showed a sneering contempt for Collier's gun muzzle. "The man is an outlaw and killer, isn't he?"

"I reckon," replied Collier doggedly, "but so long as he is in the Outpost he'll stand trial for his crimes."

Dissenting voices lifted against the night.

"This rope will be trial enough," insisted Gulistan.

The drum-roll of hoofs sent ringing echoes up and down the street. A dozen riders stormed into view, skidding their lathered horses to a halt near the rear of the bank.

The crowd split to let two of the riders who

148

wore deputy stars on their checkered shirts pass through.

"No luck," said Jock Engle, and the other deputy, Brice Fette, nodding his saturnine agreement. "We lost the rest of that outlaw bunch in the timber."

"We'll get every man out in the mornin' then," said Esmond, his lantern jaw thrust forward pugnaciously. "The trail may be cold by then but we'll follow it. That money's got to be recovered or the bank will be in one helluva fix."

"Isn't that what I told you, Esmond?" snapped Reed as one of the deputies covered him with a drawn gun.

"Why not try makin' Reed tell where his pards went with the dinero?" queried Gulistan. "I know a few Indian tricks that'd make a stone talk for half an hour." He glanced over his shoulder and gestured to Esmond, Ormand and the others. "Come on! Rush him!"

"Engle! Fette!" yelled Collier. "Keep 'em off!"

Men were closing in on Reed. Hard blows raked his face. He fought back viciously. He caught one man on the jaw and knocked him backwards into three more men charging

149

forward. All four men went down in a threshing tangle of arms and legs. Then Brice Fette came up beside Reed to brace the crowd with a cocked six-gun.

"Don't be fools!" cried Collier fiercely. "There's been enough killing for one night, but there'll be more if you gents don't calm down. Come along, Fette and Engle."

There was a fanatical gleam in the grizzled sheriff's eyes, a rocklike quality about his stubborn jaw. He looked ready to go to any lengths to stop the crowd from their unholy purpose. Gulistan, with his own gun coming out of leather, saw that and hesitated briefly. Behind him the others had momentarily halted.

Collier took that opportunity to gesture to his deputies. They formed a flying wedge with Jim Reed at its center and shouldered through the mob which broke reluctantly. They slammed past Gulistan. Reed yelled at the rancher.

"Gulistan," he said, and each word was clipped and harsh, "when I get out of here I'll remember how anxious you were to see an innocent man hang. That goes for you, too, Esmond!"

"It won't be a long memory," shouted

Gulistan, "if we bust down the jail around you."

Reed's features were bleak and a muscle kept stirring at the shelving corner of his jaw. There was stark menace in that crowd and he knew that the danger was not past.

Indecision had gripped Gulistan and the hostile townsmen when they'd had to make the hard choice of shooting down three lawmen to get at the man they sought to hang. As furious as they were, they hadn't been prepared to go that far. But Reed knew it wouldn't take much to plunge over the deep end. A few more drinks in their bellies, the right word from the right man to inflame their reason and chaos would be loosed upon the town.

Reed could resist with all the force of his indomitable will, but his chances of survival grew dimmer with each passing moment, and the flimsy protection of a jail cell and a sheriff's gun brought no hope.

It wasn't that he feared death, for it had been his saddle mate on too many lonely manhunts. It was the thought that he was destined to leave this life without a chance to fight back.

Give him a gun and he'd face any kind of odds and let hot lead do all his talking for him.

He'd take company to hell with him, then die without any regrets—because every man had a number and you couldn't dodge your number when it came up, but you could go out resisting the elements that sought to destroy you.

12

REED and Collier and the two deputies reached the jail in a stumbling run. Collier kicked the door open and they piled inside. Some of the crowd were close on their heels and Brice Fette, the last man past the door, slammed it shut and dropped the heavy bar into its hasps to barricade it.

"It won't do any good, Collier. We'll be back to bust it down!" one man yelled.

Collier went to the window and watched the mob milling in the dust. Slowly some of the men began to drift into the Palomino Saloon. Collier, his manner worried and nervous, swung away from the window.

"Fette, you and Engle grab a pair of shotguns and stand guard outside. I don't like the looks of this. We're not out of the woods yet. That bunch is tankin' up on more redeye."

The deputies shrugged, flung resentful glances at Reed who was shoved down the cell-block and pushed into the cell adjoining Jack Braley, then stomped outside. Braley rose from his cot and came to the bars. His tough visage was amused and insolent.

"Welcome, brother Reed," he said. "Your luck turned." The outlaw let his glance slide past Reed to the sheriff. "From what I've heard in all the shouting, Reed must have ramrodded my gang in pullin' that bank job."

Collier scowled, hefting the big Colt in his hand. His upper lip kept twitching in nervousness.

"Yeah. They got fifty thousand dollars and killed the cashier. Stuart managed to knock Reed out with a lucky shot before he died."

Braley rocked back on his heels, holding to the bars. He was tough and arrogant, and nothing disturbed the cool serenity of his manner. He had a huge capacity for enjoying life's gambles. He looked like a man who could laugh at death, yet also laugh while he shot you in the back. There was that conflicting nature showing in his untamed features, in the tawny calculating eyes.

Now he looked at Reed and his manner changed. It was for Collier's benefit, but only Reed and Braley knew that. The outlaw snarled and lashed his talk at Reed.

"Too bad that cashier didn't kill you, Reed."

He listened a moment to the hard run of talk in the street. "If that mob doesn't finish you, I'll do it myself when I get the chance, you damned traitor." He smiled wickedly at Reed. "You hear that mob? They're hungry for your blood. How do you think it will feel to be hung?"

Reed faced Braley across the corridor that separated their cells and his flat voice and narrowed eyes masked the inner turmoil that was turning his stomach inside out.

"I'll let you know after they put the rope around my neck," he said and let it go at that.

Several riders raced in from the hills at a dead run. Feeling was building up and the shouting became more intense. In a little while now the crowd would storm the jail.

Collier stalked to the window and peered out. When he wheeled back toward the cell-block his face was grave. But Braley managed to find some humor in the situation.

"This ought to be good," he observed. "Reed, right now you remind me of a gent playin' poker and caught in a big jacked-up pot without even openers. That crowd's got aces and you'll never bluff them out."

Reed matched his grin. It was an altogether

rough gesture that brought out the wildness so deeply rooted within him.

"Maybe," he admitted. "But did you ever figure that the mob might really work up to a mass hangin' mood and let you swing on the same tree with me? Don't forget they're your bunch—those outlaws. It's somethin' to think about."

A dark and unreadable expression crossed Braley's face. It might have been fear. It might have been just plain shock. Reed could not be sure, but some of the amused insolence went out of Braley's talk.

"Very smart, friend," he admitted. "Suppose we both check and see if the sheriff can call the crowd's bet. Collier, do your stuff and save our hides. I'd hate to stretch hemp without havin' a chance to spill some of Reed's blood."

Suddenly Braley was laughing again. Collier looked at him as if he thought the outlaw were crazy, then his temper snapped.

"Button your lip, damn you!" he fumed.

He turned quickly when a loud roar of sound filled the street. Boots thumped the dust, approaching the jail.

Brice Fette's voice, teetering on the edge of

hysteria, beat against the rising clamor of shouts and yells.

"Clear out! I don't want to shoot any of you."

"Step down, then," yelled Brad Gulistan.

Knuckles rapped on the door as Jake Engle summoned the sheriff. The lawman lifted the huge bolt, opened the door a notch. The deputy stuck his face in the small opening.

"They're gettin' uglier by the minute," he reported dolefully. "What'll we do if they rush the jail?"

"Bluff them off with your scatterguns."

"And if they don't bluff?"

Collier appeared to consider that question with a strict and careful attention. He peered distastefully at Reed, then snorted.

"Why, hell, then they can have him!" The sheriff began closing the door. "Do your best to hold 'em."

Collier slammed the portal, dropped the heavy bar in place and his shoulders lost their staightness. He looked like a weary, disgruntled and bewildered man. Reed called to him down the corridor.

"You sing a different tune when the chips are down, sheriff."

157

Collier looked up, tugged nervously at his frayed mustache.

"Yeah," he said. "I wear a star and I'll do all I can to live up to it. But when it comes to shootin' down innocent men to save the hide of a damned orphan-maker, I draw the line."

The noise in the street kept growing. An occasional gunshot drilled the night air.

"I give 'em ten minutes more," observed Jack Braley, cocking his head in a listening posture and squinting angularly at Reed.

"Ten minutes," repeated Reed while desperation was slowly sifting into every sinew of his powerful frame.

He was being crowded to the wall and he could find no quarter anywhere. Yet it was at moments like this that he was most dangerous.

Caught in a terrible undertow of evil, he refused to relinquish hope. His will to resist became a compelling force, turning his mind crystal-clear and sharp, restive and scheming.

"Ten minutes," he murmured and let his voice carry to the sheriff. "Just long enough to pack away a bite of grub. Say, Collier, as long as you're about to hand me over to the wolves, how about gettin' me somethin' to eat?"

The sheriff stirred away from the front office

and strolled to the cell-block entrance. He stared incredulously, suspiciously at Reed. Reed's blood was roaring in his veins and he was impatient for Collier's answer.

"Man, are you crazy to be thinkin' of eats when you may be dead within the next quarter hour?" Collier asked.

Reed grinned, though it was a difficult gesture.

"I never eat unless I'm hungry," he insisted. "I'm hungry now. If you're worried about bein' paid, I'll—"

"I'm not leavin' this place now," interrupted Collier. "But if you're really hungry, you're plumb welcome to what's on my desk." He gestured to a metal tray covered by a cloth. "I ordered beef and beans an hour ago. It's cold now, but—"

"Bring it on," said Reed. His voice was over-eager and his eyes were dark and brilliant.

The sheriff moved to the desk, picked up the tray and started toward the cell-block. He stopped once as another loud yell issued from the street. Fette was warning the crowd back with his shotgun. Reed held his breath. He didn't realize how tightly he was gripping the bars until he stared at his hands and saw that the pressure of his hold had driven the blood from his fingers.

Collier reached the cell, set the tray on the floor and drew out a key-filled metal ring from his pocket. Selecting a key, he inserted it into the lock of the small wicket especially used for passing food to prisoners. He had the wicket open and was shoving the tray through the aperture when pandemonium broke out in the street.

A gun boomed three times in succession. Then Brad Gulistan and Val Ormand were shrilling above the din.

"Let's go, men!"

Fette screamed a warning. Rushing boots were a thunderous beat upon the blank walls, then the crowd was scuffling with Fette and Engle.

"We've got Fette and Engle!" Gulistan shrilled after a moment. "Bring on that battering ram!"

For just an instant the rush of boots across the street had held Collier still. Then he started to pivot away from Reed's cell. But Reed came against the bars, shot his arms through the wicket and knocked the tray out of the sheriff's hands.

160

Reed got a grip on one of Collier's arms, hauled the sheriff toward him. The sheriff swayed, off balance, clawing out his Colt. It flamed. A bullet plowed into the ceiling. Then he dropped the gun, squirming to fight free of a strangle hold as Reed pulled him back and dropped his right arm around his neck.

Working with a speed born of desperation, Reed rammed the sheriff against the cell, driving the hard bones of his forearm into Collier's windpipe. Collier threshed convulsively, then his eyes distended and his body slowly went limp. Reed released his arm, but supported Collier while he appropriated the key ring.

Reed tried three keys before he found one that fitted his cell door. Coming out into the corridor, he felt the entire building shake under the impact of a log butting against the front door. He saw the heavy planks tremble, saw the stout bar lift up in its strong cradle, then fall into place again.

Swiftly he dragged the sheriff's limp form inside the cell. Picking up Collier's gun, he thrust it in his holster. Twice more the front door buckled under the jolt of that battering ram. A fourth time one of the panels split and the butt of the heavy locust pole being used by the crowd as a ram burst through.

A man's head came into view. He spotted Reed ducking toward the rear of the jail.

"There goes Reed now!"

The man tried to thrust an arm through the opening, but Reed drove him back with two fast shots from Collier's gun. Turning, he raced to the oak door, unlocked it and stepped outside.

The light of a half moon filled the alley with a milky white brilliance. As Reed plunged from the jail two men came down the side alley and rounded the corner. They saw Reed and sounded the alarm.

The tall man nearest Reed made a frantic grab for his gun. Reed lowered his head, leaped from the jail steps and charged. He butted the man off his feet, his head striking the fellow's chest, pushing him over backward.

A gun roared in the second man's hand. Reed felt the wicked whisper of a bullet. Then he swung aside, his own gun reversed in his fist. He clubbed the man on the temple, vaulted over his falling body and lunged toward the ramshackle barn several yards away.

He wasn't even sure there were horses inside

the barn but he had to take the risk. The black gloom of the entrance swallowed him and he heard the stamping of animal hoofs. The first horse he came to was saddled. Reed's hand on the sleek, sweaty side told him he had recently been ridden and that the rider, evidently one of the deputies, hadn't taken time to take off the rig in the excitement of the mob's demonstration.

Swinging aboard, he reined the animal around, seeking a rear exit from the stable. There was none. Grimly he spurred the sweaty bay out into the open.

A bunch of men stormed through the alley beside the jail. They began milling around the prone shapes of the two men Reed had downed. Then the drum-roll of the bay's hoofs jerked at their attention, pulling everyone around.

"There he goes now!" shouted Gulistan.

Reed fired once over the heads of the crowd, sending everyone scampering out of the line of fire. Body bent low over the saddle, his slashing spurs urging every bit of speed out of the bay, Reed struck off down the rutted rear street, heading for a line of trees a hundred yards away.

Guns crashed behind him, filling the night

163

with their flat, ominous reports. The crowd was a black wave moving toward him and punctuated by the ruddy glow of muzzle flares.

Reed had traveled fifty of the hundred yards when someone got a rifle going. The first bullet winged past him. But it came close enough so that he heard the high, angry whine of its passage. Then twenty feet from the trees the rifle chattered again.

A hot poker seemed to pierce Reed's side to twist and turn in his flesh. The smashing impact of that high-powered slug tearing through his body beneath the ribs flung him against the saddle-horn.

Sudden nausea gripped him, but he swerved the bay into the trees and kept going. Six-guns were still crashing and flaming behind him. Though he was out of range now, that rifle kept blasting, sending hot metal across the fringe of timber that sheltered him.

Pursuit was forming rapidly. He could hear the wild yelling that told of men running to their horses and lining out after him. Most of those riders would have fresh mounts, while he was stuck with a horse that had already traveled many miles. How long he could hope to keep ahead of the posse Reed did not know. It was something he didn't want to think about at the moment.

Pain drilled through Reed's body in a hot, liquid tide. His ribs seemed to be on fire. A hollow emptiness began to creep into his arms and legs. The bay crested a low rise, followed the edge of a meadow for a quarter mile until they hit another stand of timber. Horse and rider had barely entered the haven of those trees when the posse bolted over the ridge top they had left scant minutes ago.

The posse leaders must have spotted Reed's disappearing shape in the moonlight, for a thin, exultant yell reached him.

The bay was running strongly, its breathing still even. But Reed wondered dismally how long the animal could maintain the pace.

He was riding due north. In that direction lay the sculptured headlands, the tangled wastes of steep-walled canyons and dry ravines where he had encountered Braley's outlaws. Only in such rough country could he hope to escape capture.

The pain of his wound was a punishing agony that dimmed his vision, dulled his awareness. Each stride of the bay sent an accompanying jolt into Reed's side, branding him with sensations of torture.

Night lay dark and solid around him. Here in the timber the crystal glitter of the stars and the bright wash of the moon coasting above woolly clouds was almost completely blotted out by the overhang of leaves and branches.

The ground grew steadily more rugged and the trail kept slanting toward the higher ridges. A strengthening wind, pungent with the scent of raw earth, drilled down from the rimrocks. But it brought no pleasure, no relief to Reed.

Time became an endless cycle of incalculable agony. After another mile, with the bay picking its way over deadfalls and across treacherous ravines, Reed found it a distinct effort to remain in the kak.

Weakness rolled over him in sweeping surges. His knees lost their tight grip around the bay's barrel.

Horse and rider climbed a long grade beneath the rustling moan of the wind in the treetops. Shadows flowed heavily around Reed. Only at rare intervals did a shaft of moonlight penetrate through the timber to build a ghostly shine upon the scatter of small grassy parks in the forest.

166

Abruptly the brightness increased and the trees slid away. Reed lifted his head to gaze through slitted eyes at the barren plateau upon which the trail had emerged. He would be skylined clearly on the mesa.

He leaned lower in the hull, feeling the warm trickle of blood down his side. His shirt was soggy and his stamina was draining away from him just as his blood was leaking away.

The bay had covered three-fourths of the mesa's length when Reed heard a rattle of shots behind him that warned him the posse had again spotted him. Those riders were clinging to his trail like a pack of bloodhounds and they had closed the distance between them. Rifles added their ominous whine to the shooting and Reed's scalp began to crawl, waiting for the impact of metal against his flesh.

The bay stumbled and almost went down. Reed was nearly plunged over the side and had to grab leather to keep from falling. His wound came alive with fresh pain. The bay was running again. But now there was an unevenness in its stride. Its breathing was quick and labored, each plunge dissolving toward complete collapse and exhaustion.

At most, the bay could only last another few

minutes. With a feeling of fresh frenzy raking across his nerves, Reed studied the rugged terrain, searching for a way of escape.

He pulled up for a moment. Through a thicket of trees he saw the booming, foam-lashed race of a mountain creek. On one side of him loomed a steep-walled butte. On the other side was another slanting wall of rock and shale. It was studded with brush and terminated in a narrow ledge partially screened by chaparral. In the distance he detected a wild rumble of sound indicating a cascade downstream.

Now Reed half-jumped, half-fell out of the saddle. He landed on wide-spread boots, then slumped to his hands and knees, wrenching his body around. Renewed shafts of pain gouged his wounded side.

He clambered awkwardly to his feet, put a hand on the weary bay's shoulder. The animal stood with forefeet braced, sleek barrel heaving from its exertions, muzzle ringed with white foam.

There was a solid crashing of horses through the underbrush a half mile down the trail. The import of that sound sent Reed stumbling up the embankment. He got a grip on the reins and led the bay. Lurching and falling, sometimes crawling on hands and knees, he made the narrow bench above the trail.

Reed collapsed on his face there, utterly exhausted. He wanted to rise and hold the bay's nostrils lest the animal whinny and betray his presence to the approaching possemen. But he didn't have the strength to get up again.

The crashing in the brush below increased. Voices drifted up to the ledge, indistinct, but adding to the general racket. Then a band of horsemen, strung out at wide intervals down the grade, raced by. They came to the creek, paused momentarily, watching the steep ascent of the trail ahead of them, then plunged into the stream.

For almost an hour Reed lay where he had fallen, fighting the blackness that crowded in over his mind. And all the while he was ravished by the fear that the posse might discover he had slipped away from them and would return.

Because of that danger he decided to move again. He hauled himself to his feet, grabbed the bay's reins and led the jaded animal down the slope.

At the base of the slanting canyon wall he tried to mount, but couldn't lift his foot to the stirrup. Weakness was flowing in over him and there was a reddish mist in front of his eyes.

Then he located a low boulder, climbed to its flat top and with that as a pedestal, hefted himself into the hull. The bay moved at a slow canter toward the creek. Reaching the ford where the stream widened across the shallows, he swung left, following the narrow shoreline toward the riot of sound that marked the falls.

For ten minutes he rode at that slow pace. The pain in his side never abated. It became a living thing inside of him, nagging and persistent. He felt hollow and empty and his upper body began to sag. He was under the impression that his hands gripped the horn with a desperate strength. He didn't know it, but his fingers were limp and the pressure on his knees against the bay's barrel relaxed so that the jolting gait of the horse twisted him slowly out of the saddle and he fell to the ground.

The bay looked around at the sudden lessening in weight, then moved forward to a line of trees and began to graze. Reed lay flat on his face, his arms outstretched toward the creek, all consciousness washing out of him. . . .

In the bleak, chill moments of pre-dawn Reed

came back to a world of pain and fatigue. His body was cramped and stiff from being in one position for such a length of time. When he cautiously rolled over on his back he felt a sharp jab of pain in his wounded side.

He stared all around him, his mind slowly orientating itself while he remembered the full tempest of the preceding night's happenings.

Luckily he had eluded the posse. But he was far from being safe. Men would be riding these hills for days hunting him. From now on he would be a target for every rider's gun. It would be shoot on sight and to hell with any questions.

Blood pounded in Reed's head and the feeling of trouble never left him. His mind traveled on ahead, seeing how his future in Outpost would be. He was a man on the dodge, friendless and alone—a man-hunter who had become the hunted. He didn't know how long he could hold out against an entire range, but the urge to survive was a fierce drive within him. He had never been one to avoid a fight and the toughness of his will, the hardness of his spirit, brought him back now to the only haven he had ever trusted—his own solid strength.

The land in this area was shadowy with the darkness of pre-dawn. But there was a spreading band of gray in the sky. Dew fashioned a glistening necklace upon the tall meadow grass beyond the brawling mountain branch and a low ground mist was rising from all the hollows.

Reed saw the bay grazing in the trees and was instantly thankful that the animal had not wandered off. He made a stab at getting up. He found it a torturous experience, but managed to hobble to the creek where he fell down again.

With awkward, fumbling fingers he removed his shirt and undershirt and stared at his side. The wound looked raw and ugly. The rifle bullet had passed straight through the flesh, nicking the lowest rib. The skin all around the puncture was red and inflamed, and there was a distinct swelling.

Grim lines streaked his beard-stubbled cheeks. It occurred to him that he would probably need a doctor for that wound before the day was out. But the prospects of securing one without inviting capture were quite remote.

Ripping off a section of his undershirt, he dipped it into the cold creek water and cleaned the wound. Each time he touched the inflamed opening a shudder of agony rolled through him.

He made a crude bandage of another strip of

his undershirt and bound it to the wound, then slipped on his checkered flannel shirt. He broke open Collier's Colt, ejected the spent cartridges. Then he jammed fresh bullet loads into the empty chambers and returned the weapon to its low-slung holster along his right thigh.

He unsaddled the bay, watered the animal at the creek, then lashed down the rig again. He mounted and turned back the way he had come the previous night with no definite plan in mind except that he couldn't stay where he was.

Before he had ridden half an hour he realized how thoroughly these hills were being combed in the search for him. Collier, no doubt with Esmond, Gulistan and Ormand prodding him, had thrown a huge cordon of men out upon the range. They would beat up through the canyons and ravines, moving steadily toward the badlands until they caught him.

They were aware he carried no provisions and that if he remained in the rough country he faced slow starvation and death. If he wanted food or help or medical attention he'd have to ride down into the foothills as he was now doing.

Grimly he slid the bay to a halt atop a wooded

ridge as he spotted three groups of horsemen scouring the lower hills.

Watching them covertly, his features bleak and taciturn, Reed noticed that the central group of riders swung around a rocky butte below him and came angling up the long grade toward him. Instantly he whirled the bay and struck off through the timber. He kept to the soft cushion of pine needles and humus, heading straight north.

All that morning and on into the afternoon the posse pushed him deeper into the waste-lands. Saw-toothed crags thrust their sharp peaks into the brassy sky ahead of him and the land became gutted by winding defiles, barren ridges and dry barrancas.

And all the while he traveled the inflammation of his wound increased, the pain becoming almost unbearable. His body temperature rose, and he realized with a dismal twinge of fatalism that the fever would strengthen as time dragged on.

Gradually hunger added its stark call to the wants that plagued him. In desperation, he stopped retreating. He couldn't go on like this and live. Recklessness got the best of him and he decided that if the fever did not rob him of his senses he'd attempt to run the gauntlet of the hunters closing in upon him. Somehow he had to get back to Outpost—to a doctor and some food. If and when he got there he'd take his chances.

Running in a southerly direction, he traversed a long canyon in which the shadows were deep and full, for sunlight could not penetrate to the bottom of the gorge. He had barely emerged from it, angling into a cutbank arroyo walled with mesquite and catclaw when a bunch of riders swept into view.

He had one glimpse of Ben Collier, long handlebars mustache ornamenting his seamed features, jogging in the lead of the group, then he halted behind the screen of chaparral and waited for the posse to go by.

Near sundown when he had left much of the barren rock country behind him and was in the rolling hills again, his luck deserted him. He stopped the bay at the edge of a wide grassy park that was like a green oasis in the waving sea of darker trees. For a long moment his eyes studied the timber that surrounded the meadow, looking for signs of riders.

When he was convinced no one was in the vicinity he galloped into the clearing. He put the bay into a swift run and was immediately glad he did. Three-quarters of the way across the glade a shout behind him followed by a volley of gunfire jerked him around in the saddle.

A band of horsemen broke from the trees to the northwest. With wild yells they started after him. Reed swore savagely. Though the trees ahead of him seemed to dance in crazy patterns, he knew it was only a trick of his fever-hazed vision. Finally, the thick pines swallowed him up and he spurred on through a narrow, dark corridor.

The sounds of pursuit were faint but unmistakeable. Accordingly, Reed rode recklessly until darkness laid its mealy black layer upon the land. The wicked rhythm of that ride started his wound bleeding afresh. The bullet crease on his skull was throbbing and his head was filled with a strange, rushing sound.

Awareness began to slip from him and he did not realize some twenty minutes later that he had made a wide circle around Outpost and was once more heading toward the badlands, streaking past the lone cemetery on the hill.

As if from a tremendous distance Reed saw the bright, steady glow of light issuing from a cabin. It pierced the gloom with a sure hand and grew larger and more real with each step of the bay.

Oddly, then, the light grew feeble. The rushing sound in his head increased in volume. The hot fever took complete hold of him. It burned out his insides, turned him dry and beaten. At first, there was just a hollowness, a weakness; afterward came a total emptiness in which he seemed to drift endlessly.

The bay ran on toward the cabin, its hoofs beating a rhythmic tattoo on the hard-packed earth, then came to a halt in the front yard so that the lamplight streaming from the window picked out Reed's figure slumped over the saddle-horn. . . .

13

SALLY DRENNAN had finished her lonely breakfast and was hoeing weeds in the vegetable patch beside her cabin when Lance Koenig, looking decidedly awkward and uncomfortable on the piebald he had hired in the town livery stable, drew rein a short distance away. He removed his hat in front of her and at her nod climbed down.

"What brings you out here, Lance?" Sally inquired.

She was wearing a yellow shirt open at the neck so that the rounded column of her tanned throat was fully visible. A brown split-type riding skirt draped her slender waist, clinging to her well-molded thighs at each graceful step she took.

"Just ridin'," he said, flushing despite his own silent vow to be calm about the business that had brought him out here.

"Never knew you to ride before," she said smiling quizzically at him. "Especially when you should be in Outpost waiting on customers."

Koenig was eager to state the purpose of his visit, but he knew Sally well enough to appreciate the need for circumspection.

"Eb Lantry is watchin' the place for me," he said and regarded her with kindly, faintly curious eyes. "Reckon you heard about the trouble in town last night."

Sally dropped her hoe in the dirt, brushed some dry earth from her palms and a careful attention stilled her cheeks. Koenig was a simple, direct man. He was not meant for subterfuge. Sally knew as well as Koenig did that only some important event could have impelled him to abandon his store. A slow worry began to form in her mind, although she did not permit it to show in her face.

"Now how would I hear about that out here?" she chided him.

"That's so." Koenig scratched the back of his head and his features turned grave. "Outlaws looted the bank last night. Got away with fifty thousand—the exact amount that came in on the stage the other day. Jed Stuart was killed. That stranger, Jim Reed, was found in the alley behind the bank with a creased skull. They also found a mask and a thousand dollars on him. They're blamin' him for killin' Stuart and bein' in on the raid."

Sally's face was stony and her voice was harder, more intense than Koenig could ever remember hearing it.

"His record is still intact. Another day, another man killed. It's about time that somebody stopped him."

Koenig rubbed the stubble of light beard on his cheeks.

"I don't know," he said reflectively. "I've got an idea Reed didn't do it. He claims he happened on the bunch as they came out of the bank's rear door. He tried to horn in and was stopped by a slug."

"Anyone who believes that is a fool. Jim Reed is a killer. He deserves to hang."

Koenig's mild-mannered face showed a trace of shock at the fierceness in the girl's talk.

"Reed almost did hang last night," the storekeeper informed her and watched a subtle change come into her face—a change he couldn't quite identify. "But he tricked Ben Collier and got away just as the crowd was breakin' down the jail door."

In anxious, halting phrases, Koenig then gave

a brief summary of all that had happened, concluding with:

"Esmond swears he winged Reed with a rifle bullet and right now they've got three posses scourin' the hills for him."

Sally was a straight-shouldered girl, self-reliant and willful and the bold, hard spirit in her came out in each gusty word.

"The sooner they find him the better," she said. "Yesterday he was here to tell me he was a federal marshal trying to get to the bottom of the range trouble in Outpost, but I guess Braley's story about Reed being with the gang is the correct one."

Koening's expression lightened and something like eagerness got into his faded blue eyes.

"He told you he was a marshal?" he repeated. "Then that explains a lot of things—what he's doin' here, why he refuses to take sides, and why an attempt was made to murder him in his hotel room. Someone with plenty to hide knows who he is and wants him out of the way. I may be all wrong, but I'd say Jim Reed was on the level."

Sally did not immediately reply. An odd change had come over her—a change she

181

couldn't correctly interpret. The hatred she had felt for Jim Reed had somehow been dissipated.

There was something compelling about the man, something that struck into a person's senses, getting under the skin and lingering there. She had been aware of his strange power the first night she had seen him, even while her emotions were in a turmoil over the knowledge that her brother had died at Reed's hands.

In some inexplicable manner Sally had recognized in Reed a kindred spirit. She remembered the square, resolute shape he had made in the street, one man braced solidly against the suspicion and hostility of an entire town.

She remembered the toughness of his profile, his tremendous courage, his coolness and his contempt for personal risk; and she remembered the way he stood out among other men, the way his presence could upset their confidence.

In those chaotic moments following the arrival of the stage with the bodies of the driver and her own brother, she had seen how much alone he was, and it reminded her of her own position in Outpost. Perhaps, it was these thoughts that softened her cheeks, colored her delayed reply to Koenig.

"I wonder if you're right, Lance."

"I think I am," he insisted and he was twisting, the battered brim of his dusty sombrero. "And right now Reed is alone out in those hills, maybe bleedin' to death, bein' hunted like a coyote."

As suddenly as the reflective mood had come upon Sally, it left her and the bitterness of her grief returned to shake her spirit.

"I'm forgetting Johnny," she murmured, her voice tight. "Reed killed Johnny. If he's a marshal I want to see proof. Until then I cannot and will not trust him." She stopped and glanced at Koenig, her eyes now shrewd and appraising. "Lance, you didn't ride out here just to tell me the news. There's something else. What is it?"

"Oh, I was speakin' to Ed Purcell at the hotel last night," Koenig told her, trying to keep his tone casual. "Of course, everyone knows about your losin' the school teacher job. Ed mentioned that he needed another waitress, said I should ask you."

Sally's thin eyebrows lifted. She placed two hard fists on her hips and stared full into the storekeeper's face.

183

"What got into Purcell? He was never friendly to me before."

"He was never hostile, either."

"But he doesn't need another waitress," Sally declared firmly. "He does hardly enough business in the hotel dining room to keep Mary Lannet busy. You know that. Somebody put him up to this. Who was it?"

"Not me," he protested quickly. "It was—"

Koenig stopped and blood leaped up into his face. He tried to avoid Sally's eyes.

"Who was it?" she repeated.

"I talk too much," he avaded.

"Speak up, Lance."

"I reckon if I ever see him alive again he'll have my head for this. It was Jim Reed."

"Reed!" Sally's voice was an amazed whisper. Conflicting emotions began to run riot in her breast. "It can't be. Why would he—?"

"I'm not sure," murmured Koenig, "but when I saw him he seemed mighty upset about havin' had to kill your brother and about your losin' the school job."

Once again Sally found herself thinking of the big, saturnine man and the vague impression came to her that she might have misjudged him. She was disturbed that he should have made

184

this gesture to help her. Her stern pride would not permit her to take any pleasure in his action.

She was angry that his image should be consistently before her—big and vibrant and as thoroughly compelling to her senses as a man could be to a woman. It took a distinct effort of her will to close her mind and heart to him. But she did, and when she spoke there was a coldness in her manner that Koenig could not miss.

"I made it clear when he was here that I wanted no assistance from him," she stated. "I can take care of myself."

"Can you, Sally?" Koenig inquired with swift concern. "What will you do if you don't accept Purcell's offer?"

"Forgive me, Lance," she said contritely, "if I seem ungrateful. But you can understand"—and now the tightness was in her voice again—"that I should not care to be obligated to my brother's killer. He is the cause of my grief, and my being alone and I mean to have nothing to do with him."

"But if he's really a marshal and trying to end the trouble in Outpost?"

"I have my own troubles. The difficulties of

Gulistan, Wright and the others are no concern of mine. In fact, I have Wright to thank for helping me lose my job. But neither Wright nor Esmond nor Val Ormand will drive me out. I'm staying."

Koenig looked at the determined thrust of Sally's rounded chin, saw the courage that was so much a part of her nature shining in her eyes.

"How?" he asked.

"Nettie McKee, the seamstress in town, has offered me work in her shop a number of times. I will see her this afternoon."

True to her word, Sally saddled up the chestnut mare a few hours later and rode into Outpost. She went straight to the seamstress' shop and dismounted, giving the reins a turn about the hitch rail.

Several housewives hustled past intent upon their family shopping. Sally knew them all, but when the first woman cut her deliberately, crossing the street to the other walks to avoid passing her, Sally smiled bitterly and ignored the others.

She was the last of a lawless family. She had some of their wild blood in her and the town was showing clearly and distinctly that it did not want her. Because this town was so firmly against her, it increased her stubborn resolve to remain.

Nettie McKee rose from among the folds of fluffy calico and bright printed material and greeted Sally with a warm embrace.

"I'm so glad to see you, my dear," Nettie told her and Sally, looking at the older woman's rosy cheeks and friendly eyes, knew that this sentiment was uttered in all sincerity.

No mention was made of Sally's trouble and Sally was grateful. They chatted aimlessly for a few moments before Sally broached the subject of accepting the woman's offer. Nettie immediately smiled and informed her that the offer still stood.

"My dear," she said, "I'm so glad you've said yes. You can't imagine how busy I've been filling orders for dresses. I hope you can start tomorrow morning."

"I'll be here early," Sally assured her and went outside, feeling happier than she had in a long time. At least, she had two friends in the town—Nettie McKee and Lance Koenig.

Returning to her two-room cabin, Sally occupied herself with repairing one of her own dresses until darkness fell. Then she puttered about the stove, getting her meager supper. Afterward, she took up a book and began reading while the loneliness of this land seemed to creep in out of the night and fill the room with an emptiness that was almost unbearable.

It was still early and she was thinking of preparing for bed when she heard the fast run of a horse up the trail. The hoofbeats became louder, rapidly nearing the cabin. Gradually, then, they slowed down and halted somewhere directly outside.

An odd stir of apprehension moved through Sally. She ran to a corner of the room, and grabbed her rifle. Opening the door, she stepped quickly into the shadows along the outside wall.

Clearly visible in the illumination streaming from the window was a great bay horse. The animal stood with forefeet braced, its head drooping in exhaustion. A puzzled frown ridged Sally's forehead when she saw the dark, slumped-over shape in the saddle. But for a long moment she did not move and her eyes searched the darkness beyond for the other riders.

Afterward, she moved to the bay and reached for the bridle. The animal whinnied and shifted

188

its position. The inert figure in the hull slid to one side and started to fall. Sally came against the horse, lifted her arms, got a grip under the man's shoulder blades but could do no more than ease his tumble to the ground.

The man fell on his back. Sally uttered a stifled cry of surprise when she noticed it was Reed. He did not move and her first impression was that he was dead. Then as she bent down she saw the faint rise and fall of his chest and knew there was still life in him. But the entire side of his shirt was dark and sticky with blood.

This was the man she had wanted to shoot to avenge Johnny's death. This was the man she had branded as a paid gunman who hired out his guns to the highest bidder.

In the distance she heard the muffled beat of hoofs. Immediately she knew it must be the posse riding this way in pursuit of Reed.

She thought, with a savage satisfaction, that she only had to leave him lie helpless and untended on the ground and the posse would find him. She would have her revenge, then, for she was aware of the temper of the town and knew no time would be wasted in hanging him. But was that what she desired?

She looked down at Reed, seeing his bigness,

the squareness of his shoulders, the solidity of all his muscles, but also seeing the bruised and battered face, the haggard lines indelibly etched in his skin—mute testimony of what he had been through during the past twenty-four hours.

He was tough and he was hard—a man who asked no quarter and who gave none—but now he was powerless to defend himself, and suddenly Sally knew that she couldn't let the posse find him like this. He had to have a chance to fight back with his own two hands.

14

THE drum-roll of hoofs along the trail from town was definitely more distinct. Each faint beat of sound was like a knell of warning taunting Sally, plaguing her with a rigid fear that she would not have time to hide Reed. That fear was a hollow, ghostly stirring along her nerves. This girl who had never had any fear for herself now found that she was tormented by the thought that this man, whom reason persistently told her she should hate, would fall into the hands of the posse.

Swiftly, desperately now, she grabbed the bay's bridle, led the animal a hundred yards off into the brush and ground-tied it there. That move involved a definite risk, but she had no other choice.

She could not leave the bay in the barn, for the posse might conceivably search the area for all signs of Reed, knowing he had come this way. She had considered sending the bay on up the trail alone, but she realized in time that the horse had been hired from the livery barn in town and most likely would not go far without a rider. Once the posse caught up with the riderless horse the hunt would be narrowed down to the vicinity around the cabin and they'd surely find Reed.

Someone's hoarse yell warned Sally as she returned to the cabin that Reed's pursuers were closing in. She grabbed Reed under the armpits and began dragging his inert body across the yard to the open door.

His one hundred and eighty pounds were a terrible drain on her slender, wiry strength and she had to pause to gather her breath when she got inside. Then she bent down again and pulled him into the back room that served as her sleeping quarters.

It was a simply furnished chamber with one curtained window, a small iron bed set against the side wall, a bureau with a cracked mirror, a straight-backed chair and a small trunk which contained blankets and a few of her personal belongings.

Behind the bed was a shallow alcove. It was as long as the bed and built in much the same fashion as a closet, and covered by a wide strip of plain muslin. Dresses and other garments hung from a round pole set in the wall.

Now with terror gnawing at her heart, she pulled the bed away from the wall and half-dragged, half-rolled Reed against the alcove partition, letting the muslin drop down to conceal his long frame.

However, she was wise enough to part the curtains and permit some of her dresses to show on their crude hangers. Then she shoved the bed back in place, pulled the blankets down so it would look as if she was preparing to retire for the night.

She had barely finished when a bunch of riders pounded up the trail and brought their sweating horses to a skidding halt in the yard. Pausing to touch nervous fingers to her long, wavy hair, Sally stepped to the door and flung it open.

Light from the front room drilled out across the yard, pinning in its brilliance a dozen riders commanded by Ben Collier. Among the party were Clark Esmond, Brad Gulistan, Val Ormand and Harry Wright.

Sally experienced a shock when she saw Gulistan and Wright, two confirmed enemies, riding in the same posse. She realized, then, how much this town had been aroused by trouble and how shaky must be the situation at the bank since the robbery if mutual enemies were impelled to join forces in the manhunt.

Her keen glance traveled from one to the other, then settled upon the dry earth in front of the cabin. She recalled now that she had had no time to obliterate any marks made in the dirt when she dragged Reed's unconscious body inside. But a feeling of relief came to her when she saw that most of the land around the cabin was hard-packed and rocky and retained no betraying impressions of her actions.

Clark Esmond, tall and thin and dour-faced, his manner gruff and unfriendly, pushed his roan gelding forward and glared at Sally. His dislike for the girl was altogether plain in the set of his hollow cheeks and the flatness of his speech.

"We're huntin' Jim Reed," he said. "I reckon you know he escaped from jail last night after helpin' rob my bank and kill Jed Stuart."

Sally moved away from the door, taking three steps to bring her farther away from the cabin. It was a disconcerting effort to keep her voice steady and even.

"I heard."

"He came down out of the badlands and circled town," added Harry Wright, scrubbing

194

impatiently at his cheeks with a calloused palm. "He must have passed this way. You see or hear any riders?"

"Ten minutes ago," murmured Sally a trifle hastily, "a rider galloped along the trail. I have no idea who it was, but he was traveling fast and headed north. It might have been Reed." She paused to let the poison of false rage chill her tone. "If it was, I hope you get him."

Esmond snorted. He leaned his thin arms on the saddle horn while his gray eyes blinked owlishly at her.

"Do you?" he inquired. He flung a hand out toward a rider near him. "Clyde, have a look around with that lantern. See if you can pick up any sign." He waited for the man with the lantern to go on up the trail before adding: "Meanwhile, we'll step into your cabin."

Sally stiffened. Her face was in shadow and she wondered frantically if the banker detected the startled tremor of her lips. A nerve at the base of her throat began to throb to an uncomfortable rhythm. She took a step to one side to block Esmond's horse.

"You'll stay where you are," she declared firmly. "I was just preparing for bed. I can give you no further help."

195

"Suppose Reed is inside?" Esmond suggested slyly.

Sally seemed to grow smaller in stature. Her emotions were strained and fearful and increasingly desperate.

"Would I be hiding my brother's killer?" she asked harshly.

"I don't know. Would you?" broke in Val Ormand.

"Hell," muttered Ben Collier, "we're wastin' time. Let's ride. While we sit here jawin' Reed's gettin' further away."

"I'll overlook no bets," Esmond stubbornly insisted. "Don't forget it was my bank that was robbed." He dismounted and strode toward the cabin. "Maybe Reed is inside holdin' a gun on you so you say the right things to us."

"And maybe you're out of your mind," retorted Sally, though she knew she had to step aside. Any attempt to halt them would arouse their suspicions. "Reed is not here. If he were, you'd have heard my rifle and it wouldn't have aimed at the floor."

Esmond paused at the door to glance at the girl, a little puzzled by the ferocity of her tone.

Sally was secretly astounded at her own frantic efforts to protect Jim Reed. If anyone had told her she would be trembling in panic lest her brother's killer be caught by the law, she would have branded that person as a liar.

Ben Collier and Harry Wright swung down from their horses and followed Esmond into the cabin. Sally entered last. She watched them tramp through the front room, roughly knocking aside chairs, glancing in all the corners. When they entered the bedroom Sally felt every nerve in her body tighten up.

Esmond's gaze swept the room. While Sally's heart stood still he looked under the bed and dragged it out a short distance, shoving some of her clothes along the rack in the alcove. Reluctantly he turned away.

"He's not here," said Collier. "I knew it."

"All right," growled Esmond. "We had our look anyway."

Sally followed the men outside. Esmond climbed into the saddle as the rider he had dispatched with the lantern cantered into view.

"Can't find any sign of Reed or his horse," the man revealed. "Ground is too rocky. Reckon he must have continued north, though."

Esmond nodded, glanced surlily at the group, then lifted his hand in a signal and the posse hammered away from the cabin. In a moment the racket of their progress was a dwindling sound rushing off through the shadowy night.

Then for the first time in ten long minutes Sally took a natural breath into her lungs. The pressure that had been squeezing her finally left her and she turned back to the cabin.

Once inside she dropped the heavy bar into place on the front door and drew all the window blinds. Then she hastened into the bedroom, pulled the bed away from the wall. Reed had not moved. He lay limp and inert—just the way she had left him, only now there was a small stain of blood on the floor.

Slowly, and as tenderly as her limited strength would permit, she pulled him out of the alcove. Straining her muscles until the effort threatened to tug her arms out of their sockets, she hoisted him clumsily upon the lumpy, sheet-covered mattress.

His eyes were closed and her cool hand upon his forehead told her immediately he was running a fever. Even as she watched he rolled and tossed, a feeble, unintelligible moan escaping his lips.

But nothing altered the graveness of his cheeks, the deep circles under his wide-set eyes.

It shook her up to see Reed, who was so dynamic and self-reliant, now reduced to this low level of physical exhaustion.

Going to the kitchen she filled a dishpan with water from a bowl setting on the table. Then she raked up the fire in the old sheetiron stove, shoved fresh wood on the flames and set the water to boil. From the shelf above the bedroom alcove she took an old petticoat and tore it in strips for bandages.

Then she removed Reed's shirt and undershirt. The under garment was pasted to the wound and would not immediately come free. Her eyes widened in alarm when she stared at the ugly, red-rimmed hole in his side. From the size of the puncture she knew a rifle bullet had done the damage. The slug had passed completely through the flesh, but there was an infection.

She thought of Doc Ryan in Outpost and wondered if she should summon him. But, reluctant as her decision was, she resolved against it. She couldn't risk leaving Reed's wound untended any longer. And if she did ride for the medico she could never trust the garrulous old man to refrain from babbling about it.

Jim Reed's life was in her hands. He was

powerless to assist himself. It was a staggering thought and it turned her uneasy. Strangely enough, she wanted this man to live and would sweat and toil all night so that he might survive.

When the water was hot she brought the dishpan into the bedroom and proceeded to bathe and cleanse the wound. Reed moaned in half-delirium. His body twitched and writhed on the bed, impeding Sally's uncertain fingers.

Her bathing reopened the wound, but she let it bleed on the assumption that Reed's own blood, to a certain degree, would be the best antiseptic. After it had bled freely, she took a bottle of whiskey which she kept on the shelf for medical purposes and doused a liberal amount on the wound. After that she laid him back on the pillow, covered him with several blankets.

There was nothing to do, then, but wait. Weariness nagged at her body yet she was dimly aware that sleep would never come to her while Reed's life hung in the balance. And so she remained seated in the straight-backed chair, watching him in the sputtering glow of the small lamp.

An hour dragged by, then another and there was no change in his condition. His fever remained and his breathing was thready and shallow. At intervals he rolled and tossed restlessly, the bed springs squeaking under the thrust of his weight.

A terrible stillness permeated the cabin. It seemed to come alive while the flickering lamp sent shadows along the plank walls. Sally was more frightened than she could ever remember.

Midnight came and went. Each passing minute was like an enormous stone lashed to her heart and pulling her down into the well of loneliness and despair.

She was uncomfortable sitting so long in the same position, but she could not bring herself to move. Her muscles throbbed and her eyes ached from the constant vigil.

Finally, at one o'clock the fever broke. Sally rose and bathed Reed's face and forehead with water. His cheeks were cooler and she noted with a feeling of relief that his breathing had strengthened. Yet, she realized that it was not so much what she had done, but the tremendous stamina of the man, the will to survive which functioned during unconsciousness, which had brought him safely through.

Only when Sally had assured herself that the crisis was passed and that he would rest more easily did she permit herself to relax. Then, after a short interval, her head drooped and she fell asleep in the chair. The lamp burned lower, and the only sound in the cabin was the regular rhythm of their breathing.

Gray light was streaming around the corners of the drawn bedroom blind when Sally stirred and woke up. Her muscles were cramped and there was a kink in the back of her neck. The lamp had burned out.

For a moment she couldn't recall what she was doing in the chair. Then memory returned to her and she looked toward the indistinct mound on the bed. She got up and hobbled to the window to raise the blind. Turning, she saw that Reed was awake and that his shocked, bewildered gaze was upon her.

"Hello," he murmured thickly while he licked his dry lips. "What are you doin' here?"

"This is my cabin," Sally replied faintly.

"Your cabin?" he repeated. "How did—?" He broke off, then added: "Wait, I remember circling the town with the posse at my heels. I was headed back toward the badlands when I saw a cabin light. After that everything is a blank."

"Your horse came up to the yard and

stopped. I found you slumped, unconscious, over the saddle horn, ready to fall off."

Reed tried to raise himself up on one elbow but Sally and the room swam dizzily in front of his eyes and he fell back while sweat started out on his forehead.

"Don't try to get up," she cautioned him, concern putting a gray tinge in her cheeks. "I'll have a look at your wound."

She went over to the bed, pulled back the covers and lifted the crude bandage she had fashioned. The hole under his ribs looked clean and there was no more bleeding.

"I think it will heal all right. I am sorry I could not get you a doctor, but you can understand the reason for that. I'll change the bandage later. Right now, I imagine you could eat."

She was gone from the room before Reed could say anything. But now that he thought of it the emptiness in his stomach was a powerful, demanding thing.

When Sally returned she held a steaming bowl of soup. Over Reed's protestations she fed him. He ate ravenously, half-ashamed of himself for doing so but unable to control himself. He finished two bowls of soup and felt immensely refreshed.

"Thanks," he said. He managed a tight smile. "I feel much better now."

"You can have something more substantial later," Sally told him.

Reed lay back against the pillows, contemplating the girl in front of him. She was beautiful in spite of the unnatural pallor of her face, the faint circles of fatigue and strain beneath her wide-spaced blue eyes.

"I am curious," he murmured, still half-incredulous that he should be in this cabin and of all things with this girl. "How did you manage to get me in bed?"

She smiled, remembering her terror of the previous night.

"I dragged you," she said. "I wasn't very gentle, but I did the best I could." She gave him an account of her long vigil by his side.

Reed shifted his weight in the bed and regarded Sally with grave, slightly puzzled eyes.

"I am not sure why you did all this for me," he said.

"I am not sure myself," she responded quickly.

"I recall your wanting to shoot me. You made

it plain that you hated me. Did you forget your brother?"

"I need no reminding."

"You could have left me to die."

"I could have but I didn't."

An uncertain feeling stirred through Reed.

"The posse was here?" he demanded.

"Yes. They searched the cabin but didn't find you."

Briefly she explained how she had hidden his horse and concealed Reed in the alcove behind her bed.

"I am grateful to you," he stated. He felt awkward and confused.

Once again this girl's presence produced a disturbance within him. She had the power to penetrate his loneliness, to build up a flame of desire within him. He knew that he could close his eyes and the memory of her loveliness would stay with him, real and compelling and intimate.

"I fear you have taken unnecessary risks," he added. "It will not go well with you if Collier and Wright learn that you helped me."

She saw concern in his haggard cheeks and was somehow warmed by it. Now her chin lifted and her mouth grew firm.

"They may not learn," she said.

"But they consider me a bank robber and killer."

"Are you?"

The question seemed to be an indolent one. But Sally's eyes clung tenaciously, almost nervously to his.

"No," he replied. "I have already told you I am a U.S. marshal. I recall that you did not believe me."

"I would like to believe you," she admitted. A shadow of desperation clouded her eyes. "I have been upset. The memory that my father was an outlaw was bad enough. But when you arrived in Outpost and gave out the story about Johnny being in on that hold-up, it was too much. He really attacked you?"

Reed's bleak, bearded features took on a tinge of regret, but he could not hide the truth from Sally's discerning eyes.

"All right," she said hastily. Her chin lost its defiant thrust. She caught the edge of her lower lip between her teeth. "I can see he did. I wish I knew what prompted him to do what he did. Somehow I think he was forced into that." She shrugged her shoulders wearily. "Now I suppose I'll never know."

"There may be a way of finding out. Someone is seeking to control all the range in Outpost and is working with Jack Braley's gang. Whoever that man is, he may have had something to do with Johnny's actions."

"By the way," said Sally, "during the confusion of your escape from jail and the subsequent chase after you, Braley was rescued."

Reed made an angry grimace. His lips settled in a hard line.

"That's unfortunate. He's dangerous and clever. With him out of the way I thought I could put a crimp in the gang's operations. It means starting all over again."

An uncomfortable, strained silence drifted around Reed and Sally for a minute. The sun was coming up in the east and lightness flooded into the room.

"You still haven't told me why you are doing all this for me—a man you have reason to hate."

Sally gave him a troubled glance. But she was too honest with herself and in her associations with others to deny him a frank answer.

"I told you I am not sure," she stated while a shaft of reddish light touched her golden hair, putting an oddly beautiful glow there. "Perhaps, I trust you now. Perhaps, because Lance Koenig told me how you tried to help. Then again, it may be because the thought has occurred to me that no man would take the risks you have taken, oppose the forces you have opposed unless it was because of a devotion to some cause higher than yourself— a devotion to a lawman's badge, perhaps."

Late in the afternoon Sally informed Reed that she would have to ride into town to see the seamstress. At his quick question she told him about the job Nettie McKee had offered her.

"I'm keeping you from that," he said. "I'd better clear out."

"No," she protested. "The job will be good now or ten days from now. Its just that I don't want Nettie to worry."

"What will you tell her?"

"The truth. She can be trusted not to talk."

From the bed Reed watched her go out the cabin's door. Afterward he listened to the run of her pony down the trail until the sound of those hoofbeats were lost in the distance.

Suddenly the cabin lost its cheer and the walls seemed to press in upon him. There was a hunger in him—a hunger he had never before experienced—a hunger and a need for a woman. This woman above all!

Her voice had a lilting swing of melody and her eyes had the capacity for ruling his thoughts. He had a feeling of incompleteness, now that she had left him. No other woman had ever done that to him.

He could remember how her blond hair fell about her shoulders, how her full lips could turn alternately soft and firm, how her quick smile put a haunting magic upon her face.

He dozed fitfully for a while before impatience began eating at his nerves. He was a man with no tolerance for inaction or ease. Slowly, wincing at each throb of pain in his side, he pushed himself to a sitting position. He threw back the covers and swung his legs to the floor.

Immediately a wave of dizziness assailed him. The spasm passed and the objects in the room tumbled back into their proper places. He got up, conscious of the stiffness and rawness of the wound, and took a few experimental steps toward the front room.

Reed's progress was shaky and uncertain, but he forced himself to go on. He made a pivot and started to retrace his steps. So intent was he on his efforts that he failed to hear a pony clatter into the yard.

The dizziness returned with a suddenness that was alarming. Reed was conscious of swaying forward, of watching the floor rush toward him, then firm, slender arms were supporting him.

"Jim!" Sally cried, her eyes wide and worried. "Whatever made you get up?"

She shifted her position and came around in front of him, her arms still steadying him. Reed shook his head. He strove to sweep away the fuzziness from his mind. He smiled ruefully.

"I just couldn't stand lyin' in bed any longer. But I guess you're right. I'm not as tough as I thought I was."

"Yes, you are," Sally pressed nearer. "Only you must give yourself a chance."

She lifted her face to him. Reed saw that her eyes were very brilliant. At the same time he was completely aware of her nearness, of the subtle warmth of her body, of the wild beating of her heart.

Something leaped between them like an electric spark, and he knew by the flash of color in her cheeks, by her accentuated breathing that some subtle force was striking deeply into her senses.

The moment passed. But it left them both shaken and upset. Afterwards, their awareness of each other built up an odd feeling of reserve between them. It left them embarrassed and uneasy and induced Sally to seek some excuse to go outside when she had forced Reed to return to bed.

Later, with supper finished and the restraint still lingering upon them, Reed broached the subject of his departure. The worry never left him that the posse would come back and find him here. It was not fear for himself, but for the girl. He explained that to Sally, but she was firm in her insistence that he remain.

They argued about arrangements for the night. Reed offered to sleep on the floor in the front room. But again Sally's will prevailed. She took a couple of blankets, draped them about her and went to a chair near the sheet-iron stove and curled up for the night. . . .

The next day Reed felt refreshed and considerably stronger. His side was still stiff, yet he could move about with greater ease and he was beginning to feel the restless surge of returning energy in his muscles. He got up and

211

walked around. This time he needed no help and there was no dizziness.

In the middle of the afternoon Sally made a trip to town for news and for some food. When she returned Reed met her eagerly. He had shaved and the loss of his beard stubble made his face look less tough, softening the angles of his jaw.

"The posse has given up the hunt for you," she announced. "There's been no sign of Braley's outlaws since they rescued him from jail. Wright and Gulistan and some of the other cowmen are busy rounding up beef for shipment to railhead. According to Lance Koening, who hears all the gosip, the cowmen are pressed for cash and expecting further trouble— only they don't know how or when it will break."

"I expect more trouble myself," said Reed tersely. "Whoever is tryin' to get a strangle hold on the range won't stop until he has every rancher backed to the wall. Anythin' else?"

"Oh, yes," Sally replied. "Lance told me that three strangers arrived by stage yesterday and are staying at the hotel. They're all interested in buying cattle ranches. They've sounded out

Gulistan and Wright already. So far they haven't made any deals. Their names are Johnson, Deeger and Lewis."

A frown ridged Reed's forehead. His eyes turned speculative.

"Odd that three of them should show up together for the same reason. I wonder if they know each other. It may mean somethin'."

"You think they might be connected with the range trouble?"

"Never can tell. I'm not overlookin' any angles. That reminds me I've got a job to do and I'm still workin' in the dark. I've got to be on the move. Reckon I'll try my hand at ridin' this afternoon."

"It's too soon, Jim," Sally protested, quick warmth and concern in her speech. When she saw the stubborn, dissenting line of his chin she added: "All right. But I'll go with you."

They went outside. Reed saddled Sally's chestnut mare while she moved to the brush where she had kept the bay on picket ever since the animal had brought him to the cabin.

Reed had to choke back a gasp of pain when he lifted the saddle off the peg in the lean-to barn. Over his protests, Sally helped him lash

213

the rig down on the bay. Then they rode off in a northerly direction, keeping to the trees as much as possible.

15

THEY traveled two miles at leisurely pace and drew to a halt on the crest of a thinly wooded ridge. Below them in a grassy park nestled Sally's two-roomed cabin. It was a steady gradual descent from the ridge to the cabin.

Above them the ground rose again in gentle tiers, ending in another mountain stringer that was studded with shale and boulders which looked as if they had been tossed carelessly upon the earth by a giant's hand. And it was from that direction that they heard the sudden crash of hoofbeats.

"Riders comin'," said Reed. "Back to the horses."

Warning sent its hard, imperative call along Reed's nerves and he had the abrupt, disturbing feeling of being trapped. They had wandered off a short distance from the horses. Now Reed grabbed Sally's arm and hurried her back along the slope. The bay and the chestnut had already lifted their heads, looking up the grade.

215

"We'll hide in the brush," gasped Sally, her voice strained and breathless.

They reached the horses in a final sprint and Reed gave Sally a hand into the saddle. As he climbed onto the bay a hard oath escaped his lips.

"Too late for hidin'," he grunted and gestured with his arm.

Sally neck-reined her mare down the slope and twisted about to follow Reed's pointing hand. Five horsemen, riding hard, stormed over the bald knoll half a mile above them. Spotting Reed and Sally, they hauled in on their reins, sending their mounts rearing and buckling. One of the leaders shouted.

"There's Reed!"

Immediately the foremost rider lifted his arm, leaned low over his mount, sank home his spurs and thundered down the grade. The others followed in a headlong rush. Guns appeared in their hands and the afternoon's stillness came apart to the shuddering bellow of gunfire.

"It's Jack Braley!" said Reed. "We'll have to run for it."

Together they sent their mounts charging along the dim trail, sweeping around thick patches of chaparral, jumping an occasional deadfall. All the while the rumble of pursuit rolled on behind them like booming surf. Reed's hand stabbed toward his hip and came away empty. Above the pounding din of their horses' hoofs he yelled to Sally.

"I picked a fine time to leave my belt and gun in the cabin."

They covered one mile at a fast clip but Braley's riders managed to close the gap between them. Colts crashed and roared. But the range was still too great for a six-gun and the bullets fell short. Then one of the riders brought his saddle carbine into play.

Flying metal droned through the air above Reed's head, smashing into the bole of a live oak tree. Reed's features grew darker and darker. He realized that their only hope was to reach the cabin and try to fight off the outlaws.

Even then it would not be much of a chance, but it would be better than being shot down here in the open trail without weapons to fight back. On and on the chase went. Each moment brought its increasing pressure, its narrowing feeling of disaster.

Behind them there was a lull in the firing and Jack Braley's mocking, strident voice carried down the slope.

"Runnin' won't do no good, Reed. Your time is up!"

Reed's only answer was to grab the chestnut's bridle, kick his own bay in the ribs and urge more speed out of both mounts. Somehow the animals responded, their strides lengthening, their bodies settling lower.

Abruptly Reed and Sally stormed into the cabin yard. Reed hauled the bay to a sliding stop. He leaped from the saddle, landing with a jolt on widely planted feet. The jump caused a shaft of pain to knife through his side. He almost sank to his knees in agony. But he set his teeth against the pain and lifted Sally out of the saddle.

Two bullets churned up the dust at their feet. Afterward they heard the high, spiteful whine of a rifle. Braley and his four hirelings came on in a flying wedge, directly toward the cabin lean-to.

Reed and the girl stumbled around the front of the cabin to put themselves temporarily out of the line of fire. Reed charged into the bedroom. He grabbed his belt, slapped it around his waist and drew the long-barreled Colt from its leather sheath.

Simultaneously Sally ran to the corner of the

front room behind the stove and picked up the rifle standing there. She was running to the window, throwing herself below the sill while Reed dashed into the bedroom.

The back window blew inward and glass splintered in a hundred jagged pieces as two bullets crashed through. Reed dived and struck the floor. A sliver of glass pierced his cheek and drew blood. He crawled to the window, lined his sights on the prominent figure of Jack Braley.

His gun bucked and roared, but the shot went harmlessly past the outlaw as he curveted his mount swiftly to the left. Reed fired twice more. He saw one man's hat go sailing from his head. Then the renegades broke ranks, running their horses out of range of the bedroom window.

Sally's rifle began to blast and Reed knew that some of the outlaws were charging the side of the cabin. He was getting up to aid her when a six-gun boomed from a clump of brush just within his line of vision at the end of the yard.

He emptied his Colt at the brush clump, heard a man yell dimly and that yonder firing ceased. But Reed was hampered by the fact that the lean-to obstructed one quarter of his vision.

It jutted out from the bedroom wall in a north-easterly direction, leaving a good portion of the yard as a blind spot to him.

Now the guns out front roared more loudly. Reed, fumbling at his shell belt for fresh loads as he ejected the spent cartridges from his smoking gun, raced into the main room.

Sally was still down behind the window, firing whenever she had a target to shoot at. Reed, glancing in her direction, had his moment to marvel at this girl's splendid courage. She had been through plenty these last few days.

Grief had taken its toll of her nervous and physical energy. Yet now she faced death from outlaw bullets to help a man she had once desired to kill. There was no fear in her flushed cheeks, only a fervent eagerness.

Reed dropped down at the window across the room from Sally. He heard the already broken window in front of the girl splinter and crash once more under the fanning wickedness of hot lead.

A bearded rider, crouched low over his horse, raced around the side of the cabin to charge the front door. There were two guns in his hands. They vomited ugly red streams across the yard.

Bullets whined past Reed and he heard them clatter against the sheetiron stove, crush dishes on the shelves. Grimly he jerked up his Colt, let the barrel sweep down until the sights notched the whirling rider, then dropped the hammer.

The galloping horse swerved abruptly. The gunman dropped his weapons. He clutched at his chest, falling forward over the pommel as his bucking, fear-crazed animal carried him out of Reed's vision.

Behind Reed came a furious, lashing volley of gunfire from the other side of the yard. It was so heavy that Sally was forced to plunge face-down on the floor and wait for a lull. Reed began to wonder at the reason for that fusillade and a premonition of peril laid a cold fist in his belly.

There was a sharp, scuffling sound behind him. Reed whirled, conscious as he did so, that he was too late.

Jack Braley was standing indolently in the bedroom doorway. He held a gun in his fist and he was smiling. The smile pulled at his long lips, reached his pale gray eyes. Never had a man found so much enjoyment in a situation as Braley was finding in this one.

221

His grin grew wider and more wicked. Yet, behind the laughing eyes and the calm, amused manner burned an unholy lust to kill. Reed knew it and Braley was aware that he knew it and began to laugh.

"I've waited for this moment, Reed," he said. "Here's to hell!"

Reed stared at death down the ugly length of the outlaw's Colt barrel and all his muscles began to bunch up with pressure. Then that menacing gun canted upward and crashed in a long, drum-roll of sound that shook the cabin walls.

Watching the narrowing of Braley's eyes, the whitening of his lips, Reed knew the killing moment had arrived and flung his body forward in an awkward dive along the floor.

He saw the livid flame-streak of Braley's gun, felt the tug of a bullet at the shoulder of his flannel shirt, heard that bullet travel on and punch its leaden way through the cabin planks. Gray smoke swirled about the room. Braley was like a drifting wraith in the uncertain light as Reed propped himself on an elbow and let drive with a howling shot.

He heard the flat strike of the bullet, saw Braley waver, take a trembling backward step and clap a hand to his shoulder. Then Sally cried a warning. Through the smashed bedroom window another outlaw was crawling. His boots struck the puncheons and he came charging forward.

With desperation greasing all his actions, Reed eased back his gun-hammer and flipped it home. But the only sound was a sharp, metallic click as the ring pin rammed down upon a spent cartridge. A feeling of dismal despair took hold of him.

Braley laughed in savage contentment and dug for his spare gun. Reed came to his feet. His arm drew back in a fast arc, hurled his useless gun through space. Braley saw it coming and tried to duck. But the weapon slammed against the side of his face.

A gutteral grunt of pain issued from his throat. He spun toward Reed as the latter's shoulder drove into his chest, knocking him off-balance. Reed got a hand on Braley's gun, wrestled savagely for it and wrenched it away.

He hit Braley with a swinging left fist, felt his knuckles connect with flesh and bone and flung Braley away from him. The second outlaw was a huge hulk in the doorway, his gun chopping down. But a rifle roared a split second before the outlaw's six-gun crashed. All support was cut away from the renegade's left leg. His knees bent and he fell to the floor. His gun went off, the bullet gouging splinters out of the planks four inches from Reed's boots.

Reed kept moving, felt another whining bullet snap past him, then notched his sights on the growling outlaw and let go. The man's dark shirt billowed. His chest seemed to bounce under the impact of the slug. Then he rolled over on his face. His long body gave a long, convulsive shudder and became motionless.

Even while he was finishing the gunman Reed had been conscious of the pound of boots across the floor, followed by the slamming of the door. Now he turned, glanced toward Sally who was standing near the wall, the rifle gripped limply in her hands. Seeing that she was unhurt, he ran to the door and threw it open.

Hoofbeats sounded in the rear yard. Reed raced around the side of the cabin and saw Braley and another gunman galloping off toward the hills. Yonder, near a clump of brush a riderless horse stood with reins dragging. A few feet away sprawled another man. Reed knew at once that this was the man he had shot from the front room window.

"They've gone," said Reed when he re-entered the cabin. "Too bad Braley got away."

Sally managed a brief, tired smile. Now that the fight was over she was experiencing the strain of their recent ordeal. She had been carrying herself along by the sheer force of her will and her nerves were completely on edge.

The rifle clattered from her fingers and the rosy flush left her cheeks. Reed saw her sway, lift a trembling hand to her forehead. In three strides he was at her side, his fingers gripping her shoulders and supporting her.

"Hang on," he urged.

For just a moment she leaned weakly against his chest and Reed became conscious of the fragrance of her hair, the disturbing warmth of her body. Then she pushed him gently away and smiled up at him.

"I'm all right now," she said. "It's just the reaction after that fight."

Admiration stirred Reed's thinking. Again he was amazed at her courage, her indomitable spirit.

"That was a close call," he said, feeling winded. "For a second time I owe you my life." He gestured to the dead outlaw. "You used

225

your rifle just in time. He was ready to drill me."

"I know," she agreed, her voice faint as a swift, dark memory crossed her cheeks. "I was so horribly afraid I wouldn't be in time. You're all right? Your wound—?"

"It's sore as a boil and I'm winded. That's all."

Reed saw Sally shudder when her gaze slid across the dead outlaw. It moved him to a swift decision. Outside light was fading from the sky as the sun sank behind the high, rocky ridges in the west.

"There's another dead man out in the yard. I'll bury both outlaws. No point in leavin' any evidence for Collier or any of the others to find if they decide to return."

Because he didn't want to risk hefting the man to his shoulders and thus re-opening his wound, Reed grabbed the man by the boot heels and dragged him out of the cabin. In a shallow depression two hundred yards away he set about digging two shallow graves. He rolled the bodies into the pits, shoveled the dirt back in place, tamped down the ground and covered the entire area with leaves.

It was dark when he returned to the cabin.

He found Sally on her hands and knees scrubbing the bloodstains from the floor. He took the brush and pail away from her and finished the job. Afterward, they shifted one of the small floor mats so that it concealed the scrubbed area.

They covered the smashed windows with strips of burlap, then lit a lamp. By the flickering light Reed reloaded his gun and thrust it back in the holster. When he looked up he found Sally watching him with quiet, appraising eyes.

"Time for me to go," he stated reluctantly. He saw the instant change in her face, the protest that flared there and the worry she could not keep out of her eyes. "Braley's attack brings me out in the open. He knows where I've been hiding. If he doesn't strike again, he may tip off his undercover boss about it. You can expect visitors. Maybe you'd better stay in town with your seamstress friend."

Sally shook her head resolutely. The color was back in her cheeks. With it came the bright surge of her stubborn spirit.

"No. This is my home. No one will make me leave."

"You can't buck a whole crew of outlaws or

a sheriff's posse if Braley tips off Collier anonymously."

"Let him come. I've still got my rifle," Sally declared. She held herself straight and still. She was thoroughly feminine with a woman's subtle charm and loveliness, but she had a self-reliance that few women possessed. Now she asked curiously: "Where will you go?"

"I'll head for the badlands after Braley. That bunch will know about the beef gathers goin' on. Whoever is givin' Braley his orders won't fail to strike again at the ranchers. If I can watch that pass in the badlands I may learn somethin'. I figure Braley and his boss may arrange to meet one another. If so, I'd like to be on hand."

"But, Jim, you can't do it all alone," Sally protested.

Reed smiled bleakly.

"Who is there in Outpost to help me?"

"No one," she answered.

"Right. There's a job to be done and, with or without help, I aim to do it. I got to Braley's hideout once and lived. Maybe I can do it again. At least, that's the only place I figure to learn anythin'."

Reed strode to the door and Sally followed

him. He stepped out into the yard, moving into the shadows. He went to the barn and came around to the front door. Sally was waiting for him in the darkness. But there was enough star-shine in the night sky for him to see her features distinctly, to detect the intimate and personal quality of her glance.

He halted a few feet away from her and felt a suffocating excitement take hold of him. She stood straight and still, very feminine and very desirable. Even in this uncertain light he noticed how long her eyelashes were, and there was a shine in her eyes he had never seen before. He realized at once that the wild, hungry emotions he was experiencing were plain on his face.

"I can't keep you from going," she said in a low whisper, "but I can ask you to be careful."

"I'll never forget what you've done, nor will I ever forget you," he murmured huskily.

He moved closer. She seemed to be waiting for him. Her face, with an aura of loveliness about the smooth turn of her cheeks, was lifted to him. Suddenly his arms pulled her in and his mouth came down against hers, hard and impatient and demanding.

A long moment passed before Sally pushed

Reed away. His breathing was fast and irregular and he knew with an abrupt and startling clarity that he'd go to the ends of the earth for this woman.

"I'll be back," he murmured, his eyes searching her face as if he feared he might never see her again and must take as much of her away with him in the indelible mirror of his mind.

He stepped away quickly, then, conscious that if he didn't go now, he would never go. The bay was waiting for him and he mounted a little awkwardly. Lifting his hand to her he rode off into the trees.

Sally remained against the cabin wall, an agony of apprehension on her face. Her hands were locked behind ber back. Her lips burned hotly from the rough pressure of his mouth. But she wanted that pain, wanted that hurt to remain with her.

She watched his tall, straight figure dissolve in the darkness. With each passing second she was conscious of a growing emptiness around her, a loneliness more real and intense than anything she had ever known.

16

FOR the past two days the Slash W outfit had been working the hills in a fast beef drive. Every available man was put on the job, and on the second day Harry Wright pitched in. It was hot, laborious work, chousing strays out of the brakes and canyons, pushing them down to the flats where several punchers held them in a gather.

But Wright set his hands a stern example, taking the steepest slopes, the thickest brush, riding recklessly into the most impassable places while he flushed the longhorns out into the open. It was ride, ride, ride—then back to the camp to rope a fresh bronc from the cavvy and out into the brakes again.

By the end of the day when horses and riders were spent and weary, when tempers had been worn to a ragged edge and sweaty, dust-grimed faces had been lashed and cut by the thorny brush, they had five hundred head strung out on the flats.

"We'll hold these under heavy guard

tonight," Wright said to Noel Hockett. "Later on, Prentiss and Boylan will haze their herds over here. In the mornin' we'll start the drive to the railhead."

Hockett, who was as good a hand with a rope and a horse as any man in the outfit, had been surly all day, not relishing the back-breaking toil in the hot sun.

"It won't do us any good if Gulistan beats us to Fenton and gets first call on those railroad cars," he murmured gloomily. He gestured to the west in the direction of Gulistan's Circle G where a faint dust cloud in the waning afternoon sky showed another gather under way. "He's had his pool workin' the last two days."

"We'll beat him," said Wright running nervous fingers through his gray hair. "He won't start tonight and we'll be off at the crack of dawn. If anyone is goin' to get those cattle cars at Fenton it'll be the Slash W." He paused and the grayness of doubt and dread came into his cheeks. "But that ain't our only worry. There's those masked raiders. Both Braley and Reed are free and roamin' the hills. This'd be a helluva night for a raid."

"It would cripple us," agreed Hockett, his eyes strangely intense, "as well as Prentiss and

Boylan. With those bank notes fallin' due in a few days, we'd never have a chance to gather another herd if this one was stolen."

Wright straightened in the saddle. A fighting look came into his eyes as they studied the rugged slopes of the hills.

"Your job is to see that doesn't happen," he snapped. "Take every man you need. When Prentiss and Boylan arrive, put a few of their hands on guard. I'll be back later tonight. Right now I've got some paper work to do at headquarters."

Hockett's broad face showed an aroused interest. Odd thoughts began to circle his mind and he looked curiously at his employer.

"I'm ridin' along."

"What for?" demanded Wright angrily. Then he saw the redheaded foreman's grin. "Oh. Diana. All right. But see that you're headed for camp by ten o'clock."

The deep pockets of the hills were shrouded in blackness and out on the flats the half-gloom of twilight ebbed and flowed when Wright and Hockett pulled into the Slash W ranchyard.

The night wind, cool and scented with sage, drilled out of the timber, stirring up little whorls of dust as it shouldered against the ranchhouse walls. They had just dismounted in front of the veranda when the door opened and light flushed a yellow path toward them.

Diana Wright, trim and lithe in a white chambray shirt and new whipcord breeches, a pearl-handled .38 nestling in a hand-tooled leather holster, came down that path and moved to the saddled horse waiting for her.

"Ready for that ride with me, Diana?" Hockett asked eagerly, forgetting his weariness, his long day in the saddle.

Diana looked startled. She did not answer at once. It was as if her thoughts had been far removed from him and the ranch. Her full red lips curled in a faint gesture of displeasure, then she fashioned a smile that was meant to be polite but regretful.

"Not tonight, Noel," she said and started past his horse.

Quick temper flared within the ramrod. He leaped down from his piebald and grabbed her wrist, pulling her to him.

"Hell, you've been actin' damn queer lately —ever since that Jim Reed hombre showed up in those parts," he growled.

"Let me go," she said fiercely and struck at him with a small fist.

234

Hockett released her, watched her stride past him and climb to the saddle of a sleek pinto.

"By God," he said through clenched teeth, "if I didn't know better, I'd say you were moonin' about Reed."

"Maybe I am," she retorted.

She heard his startled oath, heard him take a running step toward her. Then she quirted her pony into a swift gallop that sent a cloud of dust into Hockett's face.

There was a bitter, half-amused smile on Diana's lips as she rode, for Hockett had come closer to the truth than he realized.

Ever since the afternoon Reed had saved her from a horrible death beneath those stampeding cattle Diana had been unable to thrust him from her mind. And the thought of him never failed to turn her emotions into stormy channels.

Because of her pride and the consciousness of her charms she had been outraged at his response to her provocative caress. Accustomed to the attentions of men and always sure of her power over them, it had set her back a pace to learn that here was a man who had been entirely unaffected by her ready and willing surrender.

For the first time she had found a man with a will stronger than her own—a man with a rigid code of personal behavior against which her coquetry had availed nothing. Because he had plainly shown that he did not want her he became more desirable in her eyes. And as the days dragged on and no word came of his capture, the fear that he was already dead kept tormenting her.

That overpowering dread had finally driven her from the house. She had to ride to town for the news. Although she held out only a faint hope for his life she knew what she would do if they met again. It was something she could not help. She would humble herself before him, for she realized that she wanted this man, and would let nothing stand in her way to get him.

She rode into Outpost and stopped off at a friend's house, staying only long enough to chat idly and exchange bits of gossip. But in that time she gathered the information she sought. Jim Reed had not been captured, nor had any sign of him been found. And the posse had been disbanded.

She accepted with casual interest the news that Sally Drennan had decided not to leave Outpost. Somehow the rumor had gone out that Nettie McKee was taking her in. But later, out in the street again, an odd uneasiness gripped Diana's mind and she kept thinking of Sally.

The two girls had never been friendly, Diana going out of her way more than once to show her contempt for Sally, to impress upon the other that she was beneath her station. It bothered Diana now that Sally should be in her mind when she wanted only to think of Reed.

Because she was moody and upset she found herself unreasonably angry at Sally's decision to remain in Outpost. Some instinct Diana could not accurately diagnose led her out along the north trail.

She came to the edge of the trees which cloaked the ridge and stared down at Sally's cabin, watching the way lamplight parted the gloom in the hollow below her.

As she prepared to go on the cabin door opened and two people stepped outside. The first figure was tall and unmistakeably that of a man. The second was Sally. They stood in the light a moment, then moved off into the darkness, but the star-shine was bright enough for Diana to see a dark blot of their shapes.

With a hard suspicion hammering relentlessly at her brain, Diana watched the man step away, then return, leading a horse. Afterward, he moved closer to Sally. Their figures merged and for a long moment were locked in an embrace. Then the man went to his horse and rode into the timber. But Sally remained there against the cabin wall and the idea grew in Diana's mind that the man who had ridden off was Jim Reed, the man she had vowed she would have if he still lived.

With a savagery that made the pinto swallow his head and buck, Diana lashed the animal with her quirt and rode blindly down the slope. She saw Sally turn to go inside, then wait beside the door, her body tense and alert.

Diana rode right up to the cabin. She was angry and suspicious and wasted no time in formalities.

"Who was that man just with you?" she demanded curtly.

Despite her effort to remain calm Sally could not quite conceal the shock of that blunt question.

"What man?" she asked warily.

"Don't deny it," said Diana, switching the quirt to her left hand while her eyes searched Sally with a probing intensity. "I saw a man come out of your cabin. You kissed him, then he rode away."

Diana's wicked manner, her proprietary manner, aroused Sally's quick rebellion.

"I don't see that it's any business of yours."

"I'm not sure about that. You never were friendly with any of the men in Outpost. I know of no one it could be—unless it was Jim Reed!" She paused again and the sharp perception in her speech unnerved Sally and she betrayed herself with an uneasy glance up the trail.

"So it was Reed!" Diana snapped.

"Don't make me laugh," said Sally, trying to cover up.

Diana's dark, patrician features twisted in impotent rage.

"I am not laughing now, and neither will you when I report this," she warned. "It is almost impossible to believe that a girl would harbor her brother's killer."

Something in Diana's uncontrolled fury penetrated deeply into Sally's consciousness and brought understanding.

"Don't tell me that you're in love with him, too!" she stated.

"There, I knew it! You've admitted it!" Diana's tone became more impassioned. Her eyes were wide, burning with the white flame of wrath. "Well, I didn't care what they said about him. I wanted him and he wouldn't have me. But if I can't have him I'll see that no one else does. I'll notify the sheriff and he can start a fresh hunt."

Sally flashed a look inside the cabin, debating whether or not to go for her rifle. She was amazed at the virulence that quivered in Diana's voice.

"You'll stay right here," she said.

"Will I?" Diana's right hand darted to her holster, pulled out the pearl-handled .38. "Take a look at this gun. I assure you it's loaded."

"I believe you," Sally replied, her lips faintly smiling and full composure returning to her. "Now what? The longer you stay here the more time Jim has to get away. Maybe your father sent you to spy on me. I have him partly to blame for losing my school teaching job, and it was one of your father's riders who tried to kill Jim. Maybe the Slash W is the outfit behind all the rustling."

The last words were spoken with a rising inflection. There was a hard conviction in Sally's talk which was matched by the unwinking brilliance of her clear hazel eyes.

The gun in Diana's hand lifted. Her finger trembled on the trigger. She was in the grip of a terrible fury and her talk lashed out at the other girl, savage and unrelenting.

"I could kill you for that," she said.

"Why don't you?"

Diana whirled her pinto, her hands heavy on the reins. She twisted in the saddle to face Sally.

"I'll be here when they bring the dead body of Jim Reed back to you. And I'll stay to laugh in your face when they chase you out of the country. Outlaw breed!"

She quirted the pinto and raced out of the yard. So deep was her rage that she was willing to go to any lengths to hurt Sally Drennan, to keep her from ever having Reed—even if it meant leading a posse to him, a posse that wanted him more dead than alive.

Some dismal flash of self-appraisal told Diana that she hadn't been in love with Reed. She knew that without having the courage to admit it. Once more it had been the old story—her desire for the pleasure and satisfaction of a male conquest, over-ruling her judgment.

It had happened before with other men; she liked to see them capitulate. When they had done so, she would take keen delight in dismissing them from her attention. Her emotions had been no different toward Reed, except that his coolness had aroused her pride. Yes, for a time she would have wanted him. But afterward, her interest, as always, would have waned.

She entered Outpost in a flashing gallop, the run of the pinto slamming harsh echoes against the false-fronted buildings. More than one ambling puncher had to scramble out of her way as she bore down upon the jail building and pulled the pinto to a sliding halt.

Ben Collier rushed to the jail steps and Diana deliberately let her high-pitched voice carry across the night.

"Ben, get a posse quickly!" she cried. "Jim Reed just left Sally Drennan's cabin!"

She experienced a fierce exultation at the startled outburst from one or two men on the sidewalk behind her.

"What are you sayin', gal?" demanded Collier, perplexed.

"I mean it," she insisted. "I guess she's been hidin' him in her cabin. Anyway, I just saw him ride off for the hills."

Collier swung back inside the jail for an extra gunbelt, then rushed outside again. Other men, warned by the loungers who had overheard Diana's announcement, began pouring from the saloons. Collier sent his high-pitched yell up and down the street and men converged in a dark, flying wedge upon the livery stable.

Clark Esmond and Val Ormand, who had been at one of the bars, came racing to the jail.

"Come on, Collier!" urged Ormand. "Let's ride."

"By God!" breathed the thin, sallow banker. "All this while the skunk was right under our noses. I never did trust that Drennan girl. We should have shipped her out of town when her brother was killed."

"We can still do it," said Ormand.

Ten minutes later, thirty men, fully armed and riding powerful horses, sped out of town. Collier, Ormand and Esmond were in the lead and they made no effort to spare their mounts.

They headed straight for the hills, taking the road that would pass Sally's cabin. When they spotted the cabin Esmond swung off the trail and led the posse to the door.

Sally, warned of their approach by the rumble of hoofs, came out into the yard. A loaded Winchester was cradled in her arms. For a moment terror moved sluggishly through her veins. Then, when she saw the hot rage on Clark Esmond's face as he pushed to the front of the riders, she showed him a deliberate, mocking smile.

"I see you are smiling," said Esmond with a snarl. Cold fury was gnawing at his vitals. It put poison in his talk. "I warn you the time for smiling is past."

"What do you want?" Sally asked without any curiosity.

"You know what we want. Jim Reed has been here."

Sally rubbed her palm over the rifle barrel. Her eyes showed him that she enjoyed his displeasure.

"Diana Wright told you."

Ben Collier pushed his mount forward. There was a look of gray distress in his seamed cheeks.

"Good Lord, Sally, are you out of your mind harborin' a murderer—a man you should hate for killin' Johnny?"

"At one time I did hate him," she said reflectively. "But things have happened since and somehow I believe in him. Though it may be strange for me to say this, I'm convinced that when Jim Reed killed my brother he was in a spot where no other course was open to him."

A hint of sadness came into her eyes as she

remembered her brother in life, then she thrust that bleak picture from her mind. Val Ormand grunted impatiently from his saddle.

"Come on, gents. We're wastin' our time here. The girl has the same crooked outlaw streak as the rest of her family. Every minute we stand around Reed is gettin' further away from us."

Clark Esmond, his narrow features pinched by anger, took command of the situation. He gestured to a rider.

"Harlow, ride back to town and round up some more men. By dawn I want the hills filled with searchers. The rest of us will go on. This time we'll stay out until we ride Reed into the earth."

"You'll need a lot of luck on your side," Sally taunted him. "And while you're chasin' him he'll be tryin' to expose the real outlaws behind the range trouble in Outpost."

Esmond and Ormand stiffened at Sally's announcement. An odd, speculative glance passed between them. Even the sheriff looked at her strangely. Then Esmond growled.

"Shut up, girl!" he said. "We've taken enough from you. Our mistake was in lettin' you stay on after your brother was proven to be an owlhooter. By tomorrow I'll expect you to be out of the country or we'll burn down this cabin around your ears."

The banker's manner was heavy and truculent. His thin lips made a harsh slash across the increasing stiffness of his narrow face.

"Bring plenty of men to do the job," Sally told him, her shoulders straight, her eyes defiant and unafraid.

"We are not joking," said Esmond. "You have our warning."

"And here is mine." Sally's voice was quiet, but the resolution in it was unmistakeable. "I'll be waiting for you with a loaded rifle in my hands."

There was no answer to be made to that remark and Esmond, angry down to the very roots of his being, had to struggle to keep from leaning out of the saddle to strike the girl. At last, he regained his self-control, whirled his mount and led his riders off toward the badlands.

17

JIM REED kept the bay to a fast gait for a half hour, then pulled the animal down to a ground-eating canter. The shadows ran thick and full all around him and the ground kept rising in steep pitches past solid timber growth.

When the bay began to labor from the steady succession of long grades and the rougher going over slanting ravines and potholes, he pulled into a stand of pines and got down.

He was tired and hungry. From his saddle-bags he took some dried beef which Sally had forced upon him before leaving. His appetite surprised him. He had an intense longing for coffee but knew he could not risk a fire.

The deeper he rode into the badlands the greater became the risk of encountering some of Braley's gun-slingers. And back toward Outpost he could expect pursuit to form sometime after dawn if his hunch were correct that Braley would tip off the law that he had not left the country.

Although he felt reasonably safe for tonight and did not wish to penetrate farther into the badlands for fear of getting lost, some sixth sense warned him to leave the bay saddled when he put him on picket twenty feet beyond his dry camp.

Then, the ravages of his day's exertions taking hold of him, he rolled up in his spare blanket and fell asleep.

Hours later he came wide awake and found himself sitting up, right hand falling to his holstered gun, every nerve tingling. A stray noise had aroused him. At the moment he could not define what it was. But the sensation of danger was a strong call in his blood.

Then the bay whinnied. From far down the trail came answering whicker followed by the dull crash of hoofs. A man's strident yell sliced through the timber.

"Reed must be up yonder! Scatter and flush him out of cover!"

Despair made an empty hollow in the pit of Reed's stomach. He wondered how a sheriff's posse had been on his trail so quickly. This was something he had not bargained for and now the bay had unwittingly helped to trap him here in the timber.

The tempo of his breathing increased and sweat came out on the palms of his hands. He leaped up, letting the blanket fall from his shoulders. Racing toward the bay, he heard the animal whinny again, heard the progress of the riders below him.

He pulled the bay's picket pin and swung aboard, wincing at the jolting pain in his side. For a second he listened and his face turned altogether grave and still when the rattle of hoofs came from both ends of the trail. They had outflanked him and the knowledge hung like a heavy weight of helpless rage around his heart.

Never a man to run from trouble, he knew he would not run now. His resolve was greater than it had ever been. He still had a job to do in Outpost. As long as he could ride a horse and trigger a gun he meant to keep on fighting.

His only chance lay in running the gauntlet of possemen. Even as he came to that decision it occurred to him that he would be handicapped by the fact that he could not bring himself to shoot riders in that posse who honestly regarded him as a killer.

Poised for precipitous flight, reins held tightly in his left fist, he decided to head north.

In that direction lay his best chance for escape. The posse coming from Outpost would have been riding in from the south. Though flankers had been sent out to head him off, it was reasonable to assume that the majority of the riders would still be to his rear.

Then, with the crash of horsemen coming up behind him through the trees, he moved off, sticking to the edge of the narrow trail. The darkness was a solid thing except for occasional patches of dappled light where a break in the trees permitted moonlight to drift through.

He had gone seven hundred yards and was fighting the impulse to make a wild bolt for freedom when he spotted two riders blocking the trail ahead of him. Proceeding cautiously through the trees, Reed got within thirty yards of them, then plunged home his spurs.

The bay squealed and leaped forward, powerful body low to the ground, and slammed into a dead run. Horse and rider crashed into the open, slamming straight for the men in the trail. Reed was upon them before they realized what was happening.

One man shrilled a warning, clawed out his gun and fired blindly. Reed saw the flash of the shot. It was like a naked yellow sabre ripping through the gloom. Then the bay cleaved into the posseman, dumping him from the hull. With almost the same motion, Reed reversed his Colt in his fist and clubbed the second man alongside the head.

The bay continued on. Reed heard other riders speeding in to cut him off in a flanking maneuver and gave the stallion his head. There was a rattle of gunfire to the rear but no bullets reached him.

Horses bucked through the timber, vaulting over deadfalls, dodging hidden stumps and rocks. But any pursuit in that rough going and in the uncertain light was doomed to almost certain failure.

Reed outran the flankers, flinging a brace of shots to each side of him to hold them back, then neck-reined the bay into a narrow gulch. He followed the windings of the defile until it branched out into a network of dry washes.

Reloading his Colt as he rode, Reed made a hasty survey of the rugged terrain. He chose the westernmost arroyo and went hurtling down the rocky bed of the dried-up stream-bed. After a mile he spurred the bay up the steep bank and into the concealing timber.

He put three more miles behind him and the

bay was again beginning to falter in its stride when he decided that he had dodged the posse and could call a halt for the night.

Once again he put the bay on picket. But this time he removed the saddle to give the animal more freedom. He used the saddle as a pillow and curled up on the ground and fell asleep.

He was awake shortly after dawn, his muscles cramped and stiff, his body thoroughly chilled by pre-dawn coldness. He finished the dried beef and washed it down with several swallows of cold creek water, then saddled and rode deeper into the badlands.

Twice during that morning he had glimpses of riders hunting for him, but he was careful to keep to the brush wherever possible.

An hour before noon he reached the head of the long, winding canyon which led to Jack Braley's hideout. He had no way of knowing whether or not a contact had been made between Braley and his undercover leader among the influential men in Outpost, but decided to wait and watch the trail for a while.

The idle thought occurred to him that there might not be an undercover leader—that Braley might be working on his own—that all the cattle raids and the bank holdup were simply the work of an organized bunch of renegades, operating under their own initiative.

Yet, Reed shared the conviction of others in Outpost that the very success of the raids, the uncanny knowledge of the best time to strike pointed to an inside tie-up with someone in a position to know about the conditions and movements of the various ranch owners in the district.

Dismounting near the mouth of the defile, Reed led the bay into a clump of trees, then crawled back to take up a lookout post behind some thick, spiny brush.

Two hours dragged by and Reed's patience was nearly at an end, and he was considering riding once more into the outlaw hideout when the echo of steel on rock and shale warned him of the approach of riders. In ten minutes two rough-looking men, the mark of their profession in their pale, cold eyes and the double-rigged guns tied low against their thighs halted their mounts at the edge of the canyon.

Reed had never seen them before. But he didn't have to be told that they were members of Braley's renegade faction. The men were quite obviously waiting for someone, for one rider hooked a leg over his saddle horn and fashioned a quirly with nimble fingers. Neither man had anything to say until the sound of another rider coming from the south turned them warily around to squint through the shimmering glare of heat and sunlight.

"That's him now!" said one man.

Reed tensed, eager to see who this man would be, for it might be the individual behind Outpost's lawlessness. Finally, the approaching rider rounded a bend in the trail. Hailing the gunhawks, he came up at a fast trot.

Reed's hand dropped to his Colt butt, caressed it with a heavy grip when he saw that the newcomer was Noel Hockett, the Slash W ramrod.

Hockett's meeting with these outlaws, unless he were merely doublecrossing his employer, pointed to Harry Wright as the undercover leader. It all fitted into a pattern, too. There was Luke Stacey's attempt to kill him in the hotel and Stacey was a Wright hand. There was Wright's odd question as to whether or not he, Jim Reed, was a U.S. marshal and Hockett's quite evident eagerness to take Braley into town to jail the day Reed had captured the outlaw.

"Well, when do we move, Hockett?" one of the gunmen, a hawk-nosed individual with thick lips and pale eyes, demanded. "Braley's anxious to clean up here and get out of the country. And we're anxious for our split."

"Don't worry about your money," snapped Hockett. "You'll be paid off."

"Yeah? See that it's in money, not bullets. Braley says to tell the boss that."

Hockett's ruddy cheeks twitched with rage. He seemed to be on the point of making a stiff retort, then changed the subject.

"Everything's all set for tonight," he informed them. "Almost every rancher in the valley is busy with a beef gather, hurryin' to sell a herd to meet the deadline on their mortgage notes."

"What bunch do we hit?"

"The Gulistan and Wright pools," Hockett told them. "Both Gulistan and Wright have teamed up with their neighbors to combine their herds for a drive to railhead. It'll make swell pickings. They'll be heavily guarded, but with enough men we can make the steal."

One of the gunmen looked a little puzzled.

"But what's the sense in hittin' both factions?"

"To make it look good and keep suspicion away from the boss, you fool! This way, when the others lose cattle, he can howl because he lost some, too."

One of the gunmen grinned wickedly.

"Not bad at all. What time do we strike?"

"Make it ten o'clock," stated Hockett. "The boss will throw as many hands on Braley's side as he can. Every one of our regular guards helpin' the pool men with the beef will pitch in."

Listening to the three men discuss the plan for the night's smashing attack which was destined to ruin more than one rancher in Outpost, Reed's face turned heavier, and the line of his lips was a rigid, unrelenting crease against his bronzed skin.

It was a slick doublecross which Harry Wright was planning. But if the weight of his gun was enough and if he could round up enough help before it was too late, Reed resolved to end the reign of terror in the valley and bring the outlaws and their crooked leader to justice.

At last, Braley's gunmen swung their mounts around and rode back in the direction of the hideout. Hockett remained motionless in the saddle for a few seconds, then headed toward the foothills.

Quickly Reed dropped back through the brush until he reached the bay. He guided the animal in a wide circle calculated to bring him out ahead of the Slash W ramrod a mile down the trail.

18

ONCE clear of the canyon Reed put the bay into a fast run and a short time later concealed himself behind some chaparral at the trail's edge, listening to Hockett's approach. When the foreman was almost abreast of him, Reed pushed the bay into the open and slid his gun into his fist.

"End of the line for you, Hockett," he said quietly.

"Jim Reed!" gasped Hockett, hauling in on the reins. His hand clawed instinctively for his gun.

"That'll get you a bullet," Reed warned.

The fierce will to destroy lurked in Hockett's eyes. But he knew he could never beat Reed to a shot. Slowly and reluctantly, then, his hand came away from his holster.

"Where have you been?" Hockett growled. "I thought you'd—"

"Left the country?" Reed supplied gently, though the ice in his eyes belied the softness of his talk. "No, friend, not while there's work to be done. I've been around, dodgin' posses and gettin' information such as when I listened in on your interestin' conversation with Jack Braley's men back in the canyon."

If Reed had struck Hockett with the butt of his gun he could not have given him a more severe jolt. Shock widened his eyes and afterward uneasiness crawled into them and lingered there.

"All right, you damned snooper," he rasped, making a show of bravado. "What are you goin' to do with what you know?"

"I'll put a spike in tonight's raid," snapped Reed. "I should have realized Harry Wright was the man behind the trouble in Outpost after he ordered Luke Stacey to kill me."

Reed paused and saw a strange, unreadable expression come into Hockett's face. It was something akin to disbelief and bewilderment. He stared intently at Reed, then apparently satisfied with what he saw there, let a faint leer twist his thick lips.

"How long do we stay here?" he demanded.

"Not long. I'm takin' you back to Outpost. I'm goin' to see Gulistan and some of his neighbors and tell them what's on the fire."

Hockett laughed and the sneer on his lips widened.

"I wish you luck. You'll need it."

"Maybe. So will you. Tonight is clean-up. I aim to make the ranchers listen to me and smash Braley and the man behind him—your boss! You can unbuckle your cartridge belt and let it drop to the ground."

Hockett scowled. But with Reed's gun menacing his midriff he grudgingly complied. Reed holstered his weapon. He took one look back down the trail. In that instant Hockett moved.

His spurs roweled his horse, sent the animal careening toward Reed. Reed made a frantic grab for his gun. Hockett left the kak in a flying leap and landed on top of him. The Colt flipped out of the scabbard. For a brief second they threshed about on top of the bucking bay, then they pitched to the ground. They landed with Hockett underneath. The shock of their fall jolted the breath out of the ramrod's lungs.

Reed slammed his fists into Hocket's face while the latter dug a knee into Reed's wounded side. The sheer, aching agony of that thrust re-laxed Reed's grip. He rolled over with Hockett clawing on top of him, pummeling him with both hands.

Hockett's fingers fastened on Reed's windpipe, seeking to strangle him. Desperately, fighting the pain that slugged through him, Reed doubled up his legs, then flung them up and outward. Hockett catapulted across the trail, struck the shaly shoulder of the road. Before he could rise, Reed followed him and knocked him out with two savage punches.

Then, while Hockett was still unconscious, Reed bound his wrists behind his back and used his bandanna as a gag around his mouth. When the ramrod came to, Reed forced him to remount.

"You won't be too comfortable," he told Hockett, "but I can't take any chances with you. We'll be ridin' through hostile country with posses combin' the hills for me. I'm makin' sure you don't yell to let anyone know where we are."

Hockett glared at Reed, mumbled something unintelligible behind his gag, then kicked his horse into motion at Reed's signal. They rode straight south. Three times Reed was obliged to halt and take cover when bands of horsemen crossed through the hills below him.

All during the long afternoon Reed thought of Sally, plagued by odd, nameless fears for her welfare. She had undertaken a grave risk harboring him and if the town ever learned about it, instant reprisals could be expected.

Because he could not stop worrying about her, Reed decided to stop off at her cabin on the way to Gulistan's Circle G outfit. Since most of the ranches were situated south of town and he would not be traveling much out of his way to pass the cabin, and because there was considerable time before ten o'clock arrived, he decided to risk the visit.

However, the necessity of going into concealment several times and riding in wide circles about scattered groups of possemen who were hunting him used up more time than he had counted upon. Accordingly, it was dark when Reed reached Sally's place.

They were trotting past the front door when a rifle poked through the smashed front window and Sally's hard challenge drilled toward them.

"Esmond, take your men and go back to town or I'll shoot," she cried fiercely. "You're not burning down this cabin. You'll have to kill me first."

Bewildered surprise shook Reed while he called out rapidly to identify himself.

"It's Jim Reed!"

Immediately the rifle vanished from the window. There was the patter of boots along the cabin's floor, then the door swung open and she came outside.

"Oh, Jim," she said. "I'm so glad you're here. I've been worried."

It seemed the most natural thing in the world for her to walk into his arms and to raise her lips for his brief kiss. Then, pushing gently away from Reed, Sally's glance slid around to Hockett while a puzzled wonder filled her cheeks.

"Jim, what happened out there?" she demanded. "Why is Noel Hockett a prisoner?"

"Later," replied Reed impatiently, pausing to listen for the sound of hoofbeats.

His nerves were tightly strung and he was ready to move at the slightest warning of peril.

"First, let me hear about you," he suggested. "When we rode up you yelled somethin' about Esmond. What did you mean by that?"

Sally's face clouded and memory darkened her eyes.

"Diana Wright was here," she said bitterly.

"She was up on the ridge last night when you left for the hills. She saw us and rode down to question me about my visitor. Somehow she made a wild guess about you. We had words and she rode off to warn Collier."

"More proof," murmured Reed. "It all fits. She'd naturally stick with her father."

Sally gave him a puzzled stare and went on.

"The posse was here a little while after you left. Esmond gave me twenty-four hours' notice to leave town—or they'd burn down the cabin around me."

Reed's eyes turned smoky with fury.

"This town is filled with brave men—picking on women," he stated, his voice flat-toned and deadly. "Sit tight, Sally."

"I intend to." Sally gestured to Hockett. "What about him?"

Briefly Reed related what had occurred in the badlands.

"I've got the information I want now," he concluded with a stern feeling of satisfaction. "Hockett is the go-between for Braley and Wright. Wright is the undercover man behind the lawlessness—which makes a lot of things clear."

"What do you plan to do, Jim?" Sally inquired tensely.

"Take Hockett to Gulistan, give him the news and force him to organize his friends. We'll set a trap for those raiders."

"But why Gulistan?"

"No other place to go and I can't do this job alone. Collier and everyone else in town is probably still out in the hills huntin' me. In fact, for all I know, even Gulistan maybe with the posse."

Reed caught Hockett's eye. The man glared at him. He was suffering from having the gag on for so long a time, but behind the anger in his eyes lay the faint hint of mockery. Reed wondered about that and was vaguely disturbed by it.

"Jim, I'll go with you," Sally said. Her fingers were suddenly digging into his forearm.

"No. This promises to be a bloody fight. Men will die tonight. It will be no place for a woman."

"But I'm part of this touble," she insisted. "If Wright is our man, then he may be responsible for Johnny turning bad. And I'm not forgetting his vote helped to lose me my school teaching job."

Reed took Sally's shoulders between his broad, strong palms and looked down at her, resisting the desire to kiss her again.

"I know how you feel, but I can't let you go. Wait here. If things break right I'll be back for you. Then we'll see what this town has to say about your leaving."

"All right," she agreed, resignation in her tone, though her eyes glinted with determination. "I'll wait for you."

Instinctive caution prompted Jim Reed to halt briefly in the timber to study the terrain below him before riding down to Brad Gulistan's ranch a short time later. Hockett was cursing behind his gag and there was sheer murder in his gaze every time their eyes met.

While he waited Reed saw a big bunch of riders pound out of the yard and disappear. That band could have been part of the posse or some of Gulistan's own hands bound on some mission—perhaps, detailed as extra guards on Gulistan's beef wherever it was being held.

Now as quietness descended upon the ranch Reed pushed his mount down the slope, keeping Hockett ahead of him. He drew his gun lest Hockett be tempted to make a last break for freedom. Below him he saw that there was a light in the front room of the rambling one-story ranchhouse as well as lights in the bunkhouse.

Reed and Hockett came into the yard at a walk, not making much of a racket. They were at the veranda steps when the bunkhouse door opened and someone sent a challenging call through the darkness. Reed dismounted, pulled Hockett out of the saddle and pushed him ahead of him through the front door and into a bright, lamplit room.

"Hold everything!" snapped Reed, his face as hard as granite, his voice metallic. "Don't anybody go for a gun."

There were three men in the room—big Brad Gulistan seated at his desk and two bronzed, grim-eyed Circle G hands. All three whirled as Reed and Hockett entered alertness breaking through the stillness of their cheeks.

"Damn you, Reed!" exclaimed Gulistan, his voice heavy and guttural, the muscles of his chest and arms pulling his shirt tightly across his shoulders. "What the hell do you think you're doin'?"

"Save your breath," stated Reed, keeping his gun level and watching every man in the room with a careful intentness. "I know what you're

267

thinkin'. There's a posse huntin' me in the hills. By this time I reckon a bounty has been set on my head for supposedly killin' Jed Stuart, the Outpost bank cashier."

Gulistan's leonine head came up and his jutting jaw worked with convulsive rage. His whole body was tense and primed for a break.

"Keep talkin'," he growled, "but let me tell you that you're livin' on borrowed time from hell. I don't know why you've brought Hockett here or what your game is, but the Circle G has had its belly full of outlaws and you'll never leave here except on a board."

The hard glitter in Gulistan's eyes, became more pronounced. Reed's responding glance was just as hard, just as challenging.

"Save the threats and listen to me," he directed. "Several days ago I caught Jack Braley in his hideout. You know about that and the bank raid and his escape which followed."

"Yeah, and about you, too."

"Sure. I've been hidin' while I got over a bullet wound. Today I rode back toward Braley's camp and listened in on a private talk between Hockett and two of Braley's gun-hawks."

"Interestin' if true."

There was a brittle, disbelieving contempt in Gulistan's tone and his patience was wearing thin. The taut feeling of pressure in the room was like a thick fog and Reed felt his temper slip.

"I think you'll find it is," he said stiffly. "Hockett and Braley, through their real boss, Harry Wright, will raid your beef tonight. They aim to steal every critter in your gather so you won't be able to make a drive to railhead. And they plan to hit the Slash W at the same time to throw suspicion away from Wright as well as doublecross and ruin the cowmen who pooled their herds with him."

A dark flush stained Gulistan's features and his manner turned strange and unfathomable. His huge frame was shaking with an emotion that could have been nothing but rage yet the expression in his eyes had changed and the corners of his long lips were quirking oddly. It puzzled Reed. His eyes bored into the rancher as the latter uttered a sudden savage exclamation.

"If that's straight goods—"

"It is," interrupted Reed, "and you'd better get ready to act. The raid is set for ten tonight. If you don't believe me, we'll question Hockett whom I've kept gagged all the way from the badlands. I know ways of making a man talk.

"Another thing—I'm a federal marshal." Reed paused, watching Gulistan and the two punchers, waiting for the shock of surprise to show on their features. Though their eyes flicked to his face, it seemed to Reed that their only reaction was to act more wary. "I've kept my identity hidden up till now, trying to decide which was the right side in this range ruckus. You can check on me by wiring the marshal's office in Cheyenne."

"No need for that, Reed," responded Gulistan with unusual eagerness. He allowed a smile to break the harsh taciturnity of his cheeks and glanced briefly at this two punchers. "You've convinced me. Carver, you and Stimson, take off Hockett's gag."

Reed relaxed and his gun barrel dipped slightly. But the old wildness, the old impatience for action still had its way with him. Time was moving on rapidly and Reed found himself annoyed at the casual way in which the two gun-hung Cirlce G hands sauntered across the room to execute Gulistan's orders.

Hockett stood to the left of Reed, growling behind the bandanna stuffed in his mouth. His arms tugged and strained at his bonds. The Circle G punchers moved up leisurely and started to cross in front of Reed. Suddenly, Carver the nearest man, spun on his heel.

Warning came to Reed a split second too late. He stepped back, trying to bring up his gun. But Carver rushed him. His left arm chopped down against Reed's wrist, knocking the gun from his fingers. At the same instant Stimson looped a wicked right to the tip of Reed's jaw.

Reed stumbled backwards, propelled by the tremendous force of the blow. Carver crowded him fast, ripping a right and left to the head. A gray mist fogged Reed's brain. His shoulders struck the wall. His knees unhinged and he slid down the wall, striking the floor on his haunches. When he looked up Carver and Stimson stood above him with cocked guns. They were grinning in wicked amusement. Behind them Brad Gulistan's massive frame shook to a consuming mirth.

He came across the room, his heavy stride sending an unrhythmic vibration through the puncheons. His eyes and his mouth leered at Reed as Reed pulled himself unsteadily to his feet and ran a calloused palm along the edge of his aching jaw. Stimson could really punch.

"Reed, you're a bigger fool than I took you to be," Gulistan declared. There was mocking irony in his talk. "I don't need to check with Cheyenne about you. I've known you were a marshal ever since I picked up your badge in town that first night you came to Outpost. I've been stringin' you along just now, lettin' you run off at the mouth about Harry Wright."

Carver had untied Hockett's bonds and freed the gag from his mouth. The Slash W ramrod coughed, scrubbed his hand across his mouth, then plunged toward Reed. Reed tried to side-step, lost his balance and topped to the floor.

"You blasted lawman!" Hockett growled. "I'll make you regret you ever gagged me."

Reed tried to roll away from Hockett's swinging foot. But the tip of the hard boot crashed into Reed's side. A gasp of pain burst from Reed. Hockett laughed brutally before Carver pushed him out of the way.

A little bit higher up, Reed thought, and that kick would have fractured a couple of ribs. But he was dismally thankful that the blow had not been delivered to his left side where his bullet wound still ached dully. Now, with Gulistan and the others leering down at him, he hauled himself once more to his feet.

272

"I'll owe you that, Hockett," Reed murmured, a dark and dangerous look burning in his eyes, "and I mean to pay you back."

"You'll never have the chance for that," Gulistan told him.

The big rancher spoke with greater composure, but as his calmness increased, the deadliness so vitally a part of his nature mounted.

Hockett thrust his ruddy face close to Reed.

"You took too much for granted, Reed, when you figured Wright was the man behind those raids just because I'm sidin' the outlaws."

Gulistan turned away and moved to a desk. He rummaged through a drawer, then came back and held out a ball-pointed star.

"Here's your badge, Reed. When you got out of jail you should have kept right on ridin' straight out of the country.'

"You don't know U.S. marshals very well," said Reed. "We don't quit till a job is done."

"Both you and your job are finished," snapped Gulistan. There was no mercy in his steel-blue eyes. He was tough and hard and utterly without sentiment. "We can't afford to let you live and we can't let your body be found. You can readily understand that."

Some of the steam went out of Jim Reed. Inward he was cursing his own stupidity even though he realized that his mistake had been a natural one. He had never considered the possibility that Hockett might be doublecrossing his boss, that some other rancher than Wright might have had Hockett secretly on his payroll.

Yet, it was too late for self-recriminations. He was trapped. Considering his chances of survival he saw that here was none. Gulistan had issued his ultimatum and the threat of death moved inexorably toward him. It stifled Reed's breathing, squeezed the blood out of his heart.

"How does it feel to know you're at the end of your rope?" Hockett inquired.

Reed ignored Hockett and looked straight at Gulistan.

"You've got high cards, but if I were you I wouldn't start laughin' or rakin' in the chips until you're sure I'm dead."

There was a disquieting softness in that warning. Reed knew his moment of fear, his moment of defeat, but to these men he showed a stolidity that was somehow unnerving. With all their confidence and sureness in this situation they showed a flicker of doubt. Then Gulistan broke the spell and laughed.

"That won't be long now. Ten o'clock isn't far off."

Reed stalled, estimating his chances here once more. Carver and Stimson had their guns out and Hockett was watching him, too, his hand near Reed's own weapon which he had retrieved and thrust in a holster. It was four against one with the odds all in favor of his never reaching the door if he made a break.

"I reckon you paid Stacey and his pard to try to kill me," he said grimly to Gulistan.

"That's right," the rancher admitted readily. "I was afraid you'd learn too much—just as you have. He was workin' for Wright, but he was on my payroll, too. It had its definite advantages. He kept me informed as to what Wright and his neighbors were doin'. At the same time, when you killed Stacey, it threw suspicion away from me, made Wright look like the guilty man."

"Then there was Johnny Drennan," Reed persisted, still studying these men covertly, his muscles tense with strain. "I never knew Drennan, but if he was anything like his sister I'm sure he was ramrodded into trouble."

Gulistan's heavy eyebrows lifted a bit in amusement.

"Sounds like you know the gal well. In case you aren't aware of it, there was a wild streak in Drennan. He gambled a lot and got into a hole. I loaned him plenty. He didn't know about my undercover outlaw connection until I gave him the choice of goin' to jail for failure to pay his debts and thus lettin' Sally in on his troubles or doin' some jobs for me.

"Once he went beyond the law I had him where I wanted. There was no turnin' back, then. Too bad he died in that stage raid. He didn't want any part of the job, but I forced him into it. His death put me on the spot because I'd recently taken him on as a ranch hand and everyone in Outpost knew it."

Boots pounded across the gallery floor outside. Every man in the room grew wary and alert. Reed's pulses leaped and his eyes brightened. Hockett read his thoughts and stepped close, jabbing his gun into Reed's ribs.

"Go ahead, Reed," he growled. "I'm itchin' to let you have it."

The door opened and three men dressed in black suits, soiled white shirts and string ties with flat-crowned black hats thrust on their shaggy heads, stepped into the room.

"Hello, Johnson," greeted Gulistan, nodding to the others. "Make yourselves at home. We have a U.S. marshal for company."

Interest quickened within Reed at the mention of the name, "Johnson."

"Johnson?" he repeated, his eyes hard and speculative. "I reckon the other two would be Deeger and Lewis."

"So you've heard about 'em?" Gulistan queried mildly.

Reed examined the three men through narrowed eyes, noticing how awkwardly their store clothing hung to their slender frames. He saw their rope-calloused hands, their bronzed features and recognized them at once for ordinary punchers.

"Yeah," he said tersely. "Cattle ranchers they're supposed to be—looking for new outfits to buy. But I'd call them ordinary hands or gun-slicks posin' as dummy buyers for you."

"Correct, my friend," admitted Gulistan. "But so far no one else but you in Outpost knows that and you won't be talkin'. I happen to know that Wright, Jackel and Slade and two of the ranchers who have joined forces with me

277

have only a few days' grace before their mortgage notes fall due. After tonight's raid most of 'em won't have much beef left. Those that do won't have time enough to gather another herd, drive it to railhead and sell it.

"In another week or two the bank will foreclose. Esmond, not bein' interested in ranching, will turn the business over to Collier for public auction. My three buyers here will be biddin' for those spreads and will see that they get 'em. But I'll be the real owner because I aim to supply the money.

"I've let Esmond and the others think I'm bein' crowded to the wall, that I need cash. But in that safe in the corner of the room is plenty to take care of all I want."

"You countin' the money your men stole from the bank?" Reed asked quickly, hoping to shock Gulistan.

The rancher nodded calmly.

"Of course. I overlook no bets, Reed. Give me a few months and I'll be a range baron with the whole valley in the palm of my hand."

Wildness crawled into Reed's gray eyes, rippled the stiff, taut expanse of his skin.

"If nothin' goes wrong, you will," he conceded grimly.

278

"What can go wrong?" Gulistan inquired.

"Did you forget me?"

"Thanks for the reminder," snapped Gulistan, irritated because he had been unable to break down Reed's firm, implacable will. "Hockett, you and Carver take Reed to the bunkhouse. Tie up his wrists and keep close guard over him till me and the boys get back from the raid and I can decide how to dispose of him—slowly."

"I'm goin' to enjoy this job," breathed Hockett. Each word dropped from his tongue as if it had been sliced off with a knife. "Though I'd like a hand in that gun ruckus, I'd much rather see Reed squirm—help him count the minutes that are left to him before he cashes in."

Reed's long lips pulled in sharply against his strong white teeth. The gesture toughened his face. Everyone in the room who looked at Reed knew that here was a man who would never crawl, who would never ask for mercy.

"Somethin' tells me I'll live to see you die, Gulistan."

"You've got your words twisted, Reed," Gulistan told him, then glanced at his watch. His manner changed and hurry got into his talk.

279

"Stimson, round up the boys. Time to ride out. There's a big crew waitin' to meet Braley's bunch, but they may need more help. I want no slip-up on tonight's work. And you, Hockett, take Reed to the bunkhouse."

Carver produced some piggin' string and Reed's wrists were lashed firmly behind his back. Then, with Hockett prodding him savagely in the back with his Colt barrel, Reed was marched outside across the yard and into the bunkhouse.

Stimson had run ahead of them and now gun-hung punchers began to stream from the low log building. They dragged their spurs to the corral and began roping out their mounts, flinging on rigs and leaping to the saddle.

Inside the bunkhouse Hockett kicked a chair across the room and gestured for Reed to sit down. Reed obliged, watching both Hockett and Carver with a strict, unrelenting care. Carver went around the small card table in the middle of the room and perched on a bunk. Hockett leaned against a bunk upright, twirling his gun by the trigger guard.

Ten minutes passed slowly, interminably, and the pressure along Reed's nerves increased. He heard sounds build up in the yard, heard

Gulistan's booming yell. Afterward, the Circle G crew pounded off into the night, and silence clamped an uneasy lid upon the ranch buildings.

Hockett stared at Reed with an insolent contempt. The longer Reed watched the deeper and more brilliant grew the shine in Hockett's eyes. Some subtle instinct warned Reed that the crooked Slash W ramrod was cooking up something in his mind and he found himself waiting for Hockett's next move with a tense expectancy.

Finally Hockett pushed his shoulders away from the bunk, strolled to the middle of the room. The raw, naked desire to kill was on his cheeks and he made no effort to conceal it.

"I've heard you're a tough hombre," Hockett said with a sneer. "Men are supposed to shake and tremble in their boots when you walk along the street. They tell me you're a dead shot and nothin' scares you." Hockett had Reed where he wanted him and was making the most of this moment; he had whipped himself up to the point of rashness. "I've seen you work, now I aim to test you out, to see how deep the sand runs in your guts."

"Deep enough to choke you, my friend,"

Reed told him bluntly, tugging futilely at his bonds.

"Don't take any chances, Noel," warned Carver in a worried voice. "The boss won't stand for any nonsense."

Reed saw how the lamplight threw the dark pattern of Hockett's big figure on the bunk behind him. There was an oppressiveness in the room, quite distinct and severe.

"Hell," said Hockett, "we'll be here all night. Let's have some fun."

"What do you aim to do?" Carver demanded.

"I'm goin' to give Reed a chance to go free."

"Noel, you're out of your head," Carver protested.

"Quit worryin'," snapped Hockett. Reed felt his pulse beat lift and some of his assurance left him. Now Hockett faced him grinning. "Reed, you're a gambler at heart so I'm goin' to give you a break."

"What kind of break?" Reed asked. "Shoot me in the back?"

Hockett laughed mirthlessly.

"Depends on how you run," he replied enigmatically and Reed felt death closing in on him, felt the air in the bunkhouse turn frigid.

Hockett asked for one of Carver's guns. The

latter hesitated, his face gray and uneasy, then tossed the weapon to the Slash W man. Hockett calmly extracted five bullets from the cylinder, leaving the slug under the firing pin and placed the gun on the table.

"There's a gun with one bullet in it, Reed," Hockett said, the brutality in him surging up from the depths of his soul in an ugly tide. "I'm goin' to untie your wrists. Then, whenever you feel like it, you can make a grab for it and try to shoot your way out."

"Suppose he gets away? What will we tell Gulistan?" queried Carver nervously.

"He won't get away, you fool!" was the snorting reply. "We both have drawn guns. He'll have to rush to the table. Even if he does manage to get his hands on it before we drop him, he only has one shot. Between us, we've got twelve. And if he takes the bait and we kill him, we'll tell Gulistan he made a break and we had to down him. How about it Reed? Are you gamblin' with us?"

A bleak, bitter smile planed down from Reed's long lips. Death was like a nervous hand, plucking at his senses. The brutality, the eagerness to destroy was a horrible flame in Hockett's bloodshot eyes. Reed's arms and legs suddenly felt heavy and his hopes died to a faint, dismal spark in his breast.

Hot blood pumped into his brain while he watched the wicked amusement in Noel Hockett, while he saw how Carver now got into the mood for this calculated slaughter. He knew just how this thing would be. He stared at the gun on the table, thinking of the twelve bullets in the guns of Hockett and Carver—and wondered if he'd ever reach the table alive.

"Just a sporting proposition, Hockett?" he asked.

"You might call it that," agreed Hockett with a grin. "What'll it be?"

Because Reed realized he was slated to die anyway and could lose nothing by accepting this hopeless risk; and because there was something deep down inside of him that loved a fight regardless of odds, he gave Hockett his stiff, implacable answer.

"Untie my wrists."

Elation came into Hockett's ruddy cheeks. He stepped forward, drew a knife from his belt and slashed the cords that bound Reed's wrists.

Reed straightened slowly as the piggin' string fell away and began massaging his wrists to restore the circulation. Carver stood on the other side of the table while Hockett was stationed to his right, seven feet away. Both men had their guns fisted, fingers crooked on the triggers.

With a stoical coolness that was not matched by the seething turmoil in his blood, Reed deliberately rose from the chair in which he had been seated, turned it about and sat down again. He now faced the back of the chair and leaned his arms upon the top of the back-rest. For a long moment he remained there, his eyes locked with Hockett's.

19

THE strain built up to tremendous proportions until Noel Hockett tore his glance away from Reed.

"Make your play," the ramrod growled.

Despite the gun in Hockett's hand and the distance of the Colt on the table from Reed, a faint hint of uneasiness colored his talk. There was something grim and dangerous about Reed, and that quality reached Hockett and worried him.

"Can't a man take his time about dyin'?" Reed inquired. "Or are you gettin' nervous?"

Hockett cursed, flicked a brief glance to see how Carver was acting. Reed chose that moment to act. His indolent pose dropped from him and he sprang to his feet. Hard hands clamped down on the chair back, swung it free of his legs and tossed it straight at Hockett.

Hockett fired wildly as the chair struck his chest, dropped against his knees and sent him plunging to the floor. A slug whined past Reed as he lunged for the table. He saw muzzle light

286

bloom from the round bore of Carver's gun, felt a bullet pluck at his shirtsleeves.

Then he slid a hand across the table, found the gun and whipped it around at Hockett. Reed's waist and legs heaved against the table, upended it and sent it crashing into Carver. It bowled the gunman over.

Hockett, entangled in the rungs of the chair, scrambled free, tried another shot and missed. Reed caught him full in the sights of his weapon and dropped hammer. The gun bucked against Reed's wrist. The explosion of the shot reverberated in the room and a dark hole appeared in the center of the foreman's forehead.

Desperately Reed hurled himself to the door. Carver was bellowing curses, leaping up from the table and firing at him. Reed made a grab for Hockett's forty-five and missed. With a dismal despair he saw Carver's gun barrel swing toward him. Reed's muscles knotted and quivered, waiting for the bite of lead. Then there was a deafening explosion.

Strangely enough, there was no lancet of flame from Carver's gun, no slashing whine of a bullet. Through dazed, unbelieving eyes Reed saw Carver stumble forward. The outlaw dropped his gun. The shock of death was on

Carver's face. It pulled the blood out of his skin, sent it churning and bubbling through the fingers which clutched at his chest.

Only then did Reed realize that the shot had come from behind him and that it had been a rifle and not a six-gun. He got swiftly to his feet and turned to the door. Amazement halted him where he was.

Sally Drennan lingered in the open doorway. The blackness of the yard was behind her, but the lamplight from the bunkhouse etched in clear lines the stunned, half-horrified expression on her cheeks.

The rifle barrel in her hands sagged toward the floor and smoke curled lazily from it.

Then her head lifted and her eyes came back to focus and instant concern leaped into them.

"Jim!" she cried. "You've been hurt again?"

Reed met Sally at the door. His arms were clumsy as they went around her. A shudder dragged its trembling course through her slender, willowy body.

"No," he said, "but another minute would have been the last of me." He moved his arms to her shoulders, pushed her gently away from him so he could look at her. "This is gettin' to be a habit, your savin' my life."

288

He was smiling, but not yet could she return the gesture. She was shaken by the enormity of her action. Killing a man was a new and terrifying experience to her.

"I couldn't stay in the cabin," she said at last, "knowing that you were fighting this battle alone. You've made too many enenies. That's why I had to come."

Reed looked at the two lifeless bodies sprawled on the floor with a vague distaste. He had no love for killing. Each time it was forced upon him the harshness of his existence was impressed upon him with renewed force.

"I've got to ride," he said, flashing a glance at an old-fashioned clock above the fireplace. "It's nearly ten o'clock. That raid will be going on very soon. Even now it's probably too late to stop Gulistan and Braley. But I must warn Wright."

"Let's go," said Sally.

Reed started to protest. But the determined thrust to her chin, the bleakness in her own gaze, told him any argument he might make would be futile. So he took her arm and together they rushed outside, mounted their horses and sped off through the night.

Twenty minutes later they entered the Slash

W yard in a harsh clatter of sound. They made no effort to disguise their approach for time was too valuable now. All cards were on the table so far as Reed was concerned.

"Better stay on the porch, Sally," Reed told her as he stamped across the gallery and pushed open the door of the front room.

Harry Wright was alone in the room, seated at a battered desk, going over his tally books with a frowning care. He hauled himself out of the chair at Reed's entrance. His manner was instantly stiff and alert. But he made no hostile motion, for Reed's gun was lined upon him.

"Wright," declared Reed in a penetrating voice, "get your hands out of the bunkhouse pronto. If you want to save your beef we've got to ride. There's goin' to be a raid."

Uncertainty and suspicion moved strongly through the rancher.

"Hold on, Reed. Not so fast. How in hell do you know so much about it? I'm not forgettin' that the Outpost bank was robbed a few days ago and the cashier was fatally shot. Everyone tabbed you as the killer."

Wright's glance was hard and demanding, but Reed waved his querulous doubts aside with an impatient sweep of his hand.

"I didn't kill Stuart," he said. "And I had no part in that bank hold-up. But I do know that tonight you and all your friends are due to be cleaned out unless you act at once." Reed dug into his shirt pocket and drew out the battered, ball-pointed star that was the badge of his profession. "Take a look at this. It's my marshal's badge. Brad Gulistan had it, but I got it back from him tonight."

"Gulistan?" Wright repeated in a strange tone. "You mean that—?"

"I mean Gulistan is the man behind the organized lawlessness in Outpost—the man who has been givin' the Braley gang their orders. And tonight they mean to steal your herd, massacre your punchers so you'll lose your ranch. When that happens Gulistan can take over at public auction through dummy buyers—after the bank had instituted foreclosure proceedings through the sheriff's office."

Quickly Reed related how Sally Drennan had given him a temporary haven from the posse, then gave an account of his brush with the posse later and his subsequent trip to the badlands.

"You've had two traitors on your payroll," he added.

"Who were they?" Wright asked quickly.

Reed listened a moment as he heard a slight clamor in the yard. Punchers were coming from the bunkhouse, no doubt heading for the house. And from somewhere upstairs he heard the light patter of boots.

"Stacey and Hockett," Reed replied. His lips barely moved and his impatience was growing. "Stacey got his orders to kill me from Gulistan. When I nailed Stacey instead, it worked out swell for Gulistan because it made you look guilty."

Harry Wright nodded. His features were tight with concern.

"Where's Hockett now?"

"He's dead."

There was a shrill feminine cry at the inner door to the left of Reed. He saw Diana Wright, her eyes wild, her expression almost unbalanced, lunge into the room.

"If he's dead then I'll kill you, Jim Reed!" she said. She saw the gun in his hand but paid it no heed. Her own slender fingers reached for the .38 in a holster at her right hip. "You wanted no part of me. I was angry at first, but I've had time to think now. Noel Hockett is the man I want. If you've killed him, I'll see you die, too—see that you never have Sally Drennan."

"Look out, Jim!"

There was yelling in the yard and boots drummed across the porch. But Sally Drennan, her hat flying off her head, was running ahead of that clamor. She rushed at Diana, slammed her weight against the dark-haired girl. She wrestled the gun from Diana's fingers, cuffed her with a small, knotted fist.

"You'll do no killing while I'm around," Sally stated hotly.

For one brief, wild moment, Diana crouched against the wall, her eyes blazing, her lips forming a rigid, unpleasant line. Her slender hands were opening and closing in jerky, spasmodic motions as if the long, tapering fingers ached with the desire to rake Sally's cheeks.

"Diana!" yelled Wright, his face gray with shock and wonder. "Have you gone crazy?"

"No, Dad," she answered bitterly. "But Noel is—"

"If you're tryin' to say you love him, it took you long enough to find out," Wright declared without feeling. "You've flirted with every drifting cowhand that ever wandered into Outpost. Maybe this will be a lesson to you.

And if Hockett was doublecrossing me he deserved to die." Wright turned to Reed. "Let's hear the details."

Reed told him tersely. He had barely finished when they heard the distant sound of gunshots carried to them by the wind lashing in from the badlands.

"Do you hear that, Wright?" Reed asked. "That's the start of the raid I was tellin' you about. Are you ridin' or stickin' here to take your beatin' lyin' down?"

Wright stiffened. His gnarled hands tugged at his gun belt and fierce resolution steeled his gaze.

"I'm ridin'." He glanced past Reed to a few punchers who had stormed in from the porch and stood there immobile and tensely listening. "All I've got is seven riders. The rest are with the beef."

Disappointment tugged at Reed with a heavy hand. He scowled.

"It's no army," he said. "But seven men are better than none. We'll pick up the rest on the way to the badlands—if they're not dead by that time."

Wright bit his lip as he strode to the door. "How about a posse?"

"Collier and half the town are in the hills, huntin' me. With luck they may be attracted to the raid by the firing. If not—"

Reed did not finish. There was no need for him to do so. Wright could tell from the set lines bracketing Reed's mouth how hopeless the situation was—how tremendous the odds must be against them. But he also saw in Reed's face the implacable will to fight regardless of the consequences. Somehow it cheered Wright. He swung to face his men.

"If any of you feel like pullin' up stakes, now is the time to do it," he told them. "This will be no picnic and some of us won't be riding' back."

A wild roar greeted Wright's remark.

"We'll never get those outlaws standin' here!" one puncher growled. His comment was echoed by the others.

"All right!" said the rancher. "Grab your horses."

They stormed out of the door, raced to the corral. Reed turned to find Sally at his side. She saw his hard, purposeful glance.

"Don't say it, Jim," she murmured rapidly. "I've come this far. I'll tag along the rest of the way."

Reed nodded in grim resignation. He gave her a boost into her saddle, then swung aboard a fresh horse one of the Slash W punchers had roped for him.

At a signal from Reed the entire party thundered out of the yard. No one spoke during the tense quarter hour that followed. The sound of firing which at first had become louder, suddenly dwindled off and was superseded by the muted bawling of cattle.

"Guess it's all over," observed Harry Wright, shouting to make himself heard above the din of hoofs.

Reed watched bleak defeat deepen the weathered lines in the rancher's countenance and shook his head.

"Not yet. The outlaws still have to get away with those critters. They'll be governed by the speed of the herd."

On through the night they raced, taking the steep grades without any slackening of speed. They topped a ridge, angled across a grassy glade.

Out of the timber on the yonder side a small knot of horsemen rode, bearing down upon them. Reed immediately swung his horse wide.

"Spread out! Be ready for trouble!" he yelled.

Quickly the riders behind him fanned out, guns leaping into their fists. The horsemen approaching them began to rein up.

"Who's that?" someone shouted.

Wright grunted in surprise.

"It's Dell Martin, one of my riders," he gasped. "Must be—" He broke off, a dull misery in his eyes.

"What's left of your cattle guards, I reckon," Reed finished. He lifted his voice. "Come ahead, gents, if you're friends of the Slash W."

In a moment the seven riders came up at a slow canter. Two of them sagged weakly over their saddle horns.

"Wright!" gasped Martin, his voice weak with pain and fatigue. "Raiders hit the herd— wiped out most of us. We—we were ridin' for help. They're takin' the cattle toward the badlands. Too many of 'em for us to buck."

"We know about it," growled Wright. "Reed here, who is a U.S. marshal, tipped us off— but a little too late."

Three of the riders, including both of the badly wounded men, were Slash W hands. The remaining four were equally divided among Prentiss and Boylan punchers.

Reed glanced at the wounded hands, his face hard and savage.

"You fellers get back to the Slash W and have the cook fix up your wounds. The rest of you are welcome to come along. We can use some extra guns."

"Count me in," said big Dell Martin. His eyes, however, remained forlorn and dull as he gazed at the small party. "We haven't half enough men to fight that outlaw crew. It'll be suicide."

"Suicide or not, we're fightin'," grunted Wright savagely. "This means the existence or destruction of the Slash W. If we don't fight now we'll be through in Outpost."

"That's the way it shapes up, Martin," Reed added. "I've got an idea in back of my head. If it ain't too late we may have a chance of gettin' that beef back and also smashin' Gulistan and Braley. Besides, with a posse beatin' the hills luck may play along with us and bring them in on our side—if they're close enough to hear this shootin' or the ruckus to come."

Nothing more was said. The two wounded men kicked their horses into motion and drifted off. The other five cattle guards joined the ranks of Reed's small crew.

They could hear the faint sounds of bawling cattle. The taint of dry dust stirred up by stampeding hoofs rolled against the riders, whipped from the north by the strengthening breeze.

When they reached the holding grounds higher in the hills the scent of dust and powder smoke was stronger, more pungent. The ground was pock-marked by a welter of hoofprints. Dead cattle, downed by bullets or trampled in the wild rush, littered the earth. Small mounds that were dark blobs in the clear moonlight were the bodies of punchers and outlaws alike who had stopped lead and would never see another sunrise.

Reed drew up, his keen eyes building a dismal picture of this slaughter as it must have happened. Here loyal men of Wright, Prentiss and Boylan had given their lives to protect that pool of beef. But they hadn't had a chance against the overwhelming numbers of renegades.

Somewhere farther west a similar raid was due to take place against the Gulistan pool. But in this case Gulistan hands would join the masked raiders, turning upon the combined guards provided by Gulistan's neighbors, to hasten the carnage. Later, deep in the hills, the two bands of men and cattle would join for the drive into Braley's hideout.

Thinking of all the innocent men who had died here, Jim Reed felt all considerations of mercy wash out of him. Rage was like a bared claw, raking his nerves, spilling the fury of his rising temper all through his sytem. Afterward he found himself relishing the violence that was to come. It was always this way when circumstances drove him beyond the limits of patience, tightened his resolve to do the things that had to be done.

At this moment he was as cold and as ruthless as any of Gulistan's hardcases could hope to be. It showed in the solid thrust of his jaw, in the way his lips folded together, in the way the words clipped past his teeth when he spoke to Harry Wright.

"We part company for a while," he said.

"What do you mean?" the rancher asked.

"In a straight shoot-out we'd never have a chance against the combined crews of Gulistan and Braley," Reed informed him. "As I mentioned back in the house, a second raid will take place on the Gulistan holding grounds against Gulistan's beef and his pool members. That's to throw suspicion away from him and, at the same time, to cripple the neighbors who put their trust in him.

"Those raiders will be joining the bunch who massacred your outfit. There's one thing in our favor. I'm the man who knows where Braley's hideout is located. Gulistan, of course, figures I'm still a prisoner at the Circle G.

"Our one chance lies in trapping the outlaws and the cattle in a certain long canyon they have to follow to reach Braley's hidden valley. I intend to go ahead with two men and take care of setting the trap. You and the rest follow as fast as you can along the regular trail. I'll be takin' a short-cut. You fellers ride hard as you can to catch up to the outlaws.

"But stay out of sight and don't start anythin' until you hear a ruckus in a gorge. Then bring your men up quickly. We'll trap the skunks between two fires and stampede the cows in the bargain."

"Where's that canyon you're talkin' about?" Wright demanded.

In a few terse sentences Jim Reed outlined the location of the gorge, giving distinguishing

301

landmarks which Wright and the others could not miss on this clear, moonlit night.

"All right," said the Slash W rancher. "We'll do our part. But it seems to me you're takin' most of the risk. Don't know just what you're plannin', but I hope it works."

"If it doesn't, we're all sunk," snapped Reed.

He turned, singled out Dell Martin and another puncher to accompany him. They started to move off. Another horse followed them. Reed twisted in the saddle as Sally rode up beside him.

"I'm seein' this through, Jim," she said with a quiet insistence.

She was a range girl, born and bred to this land's wildness—a woman who would never hesitate to fight for her own with whatever weapons were at hand. Now, she was thinking of Johnny who had died because of Brad Gulistan's greed for power, recalling the little details of Johnny's downfall which Reed had revealed to her after his escape from death at the Circle G.

But more than anything else, she was thinking of Jim Reed, whose iron will and lonely existence were so much like her own. She had lost one of her men. If she had to lose another, she meant to die fighting at his side.

These were the unsaid things in her eyes. Reed looked at her and understood this girl as no other man could have understood her. What he saw in her eyes kindled a warm flame inside of him.

"Sure you are, Sally," he murmured. "Let's ride."

Dell Martin smothered a protest of surprise, gazing in silent admiration at the girl. His eyes met the other rider's. Both men shrugged, then lashed their mounts into a gallop as Reed and Sally led the way out from the meadow into a steep side-trail in the timber.

Behind them they heard Wright gather his crew and follow the clearly defined imprints of the driven cattle.

Reed set a blistering pace over terrain that grew more rugged with each passing mile. The land was cut by eroded barrancas, patches of catclaw and mazanita and prickly pear which had to be by-passed.

At one time they heard the bawling of cattle, the distant yells of men herding steers onward.

"Braley and Gulistan are only a few miles east of us," Reed said. "We've got a hard ride ahead of us and a long climb to the top of a mesa where I plan to set my trap. But I think we'll make it."

They hammered on, pursuing a steep-walled arroyo for two miles, then switching into a stand of timber that grew more sparse as the trail lifted steadily toward the crest of a ridge.

Their horses were blowing hard when they reached the rendezvous spot kept by Noel Hockett and Braley's gunmen. Here they pulled up. Far to the rear they could hear only a faint murmur of sound, indicating the approach of a big band of cattle and horses and men.

"Where do we go from here?" Dell Martin inquired tensely.

Reed gestured toward the narrow path that wandered up along the canyon wall like a twisted thread.

"We take that trail to the top of the mesa."

"Hell," said Martin, "it doesn't look wide enough for a mountain goat."

"It's wide enough," Reed retorted. "Come along."

He kicked his roan forward and up the first steep slant of the ledge trail. Sally guided her mount in behind the roan. Martin and the other man followed closely.

On a moonless night this climb would have been suicidal. Even so, once the moon had passed its zenith in the sky, much of the canyon wall would be left in impenetrable shadow. To proceed in darkness with a rocky precipice on one side and empty space on the other, would be a perilous venture.

It was this thought which prompted Reed to push the roan along at a pace that actually invited disaster. Loose stones and shale clattered under their ponies' feet, skidded over the edge of the trail to go bouncing down into the gorge.

Once the bay stumbled, slid toward the rim. Sally cried out in fear. But Reed's iron hand on the reins swung the roan back, forefeet grappling for a fresh hold on the path.

"Better take it easy," cautioned Dell Martin. The thin, high note of worry was in his tone. "If I have to die I'd rather it was with a bullet in my gizzard."

Reed didn't turn around, but his voice floated back to Martin, crisp and unrelenting.

"That moon won't stay where it is all night. We'll need its light comin' down again. There's work to be done on the mesa. If we take too much time doin' it, we'll be marooned up there while Harry Wright and the others face those outlaws alone."

They reached the high plateau fifteen minutes later and halted.

"I'm glad that's over," said Martin with a sigh of relief.

It was cooler here. A brisk wind lashed down from the higher peaks, carrying with it the sweet scent of sage. They rested ten minutes until the rumble of hoofs, the bawling of cattle being pushed at a rapid rate of speed, was borne to them by the breeze.

"Time to move on," said Reed. "We don't want to be spotted here. It's important that those cattle and men get well into the gorge before we pull our little surprise."

Reed wheeled the roan about and cantered off across the flat, boulder-strewn tableland. He angled away from the canyon rim, not wishing to be skylined for the riders who would soon come into view below them.

They rode a mile and a half up-canyon before Reed called a halt and dismounted near a huge nest of rocks. Without a word the others swung down from their saddles.

"Sally, your job is to watch the horses and stay away from the cliff edge."

The girl nodded, taking the reins of the animals and leading them off a hundred yards or so.

Martin let his shrewd, speculative glance linger upon the rubble of rocks that littered the canyon rim.

"You figurin' on blockin' the canyon with a landslide?"

"Yeah." Reed's answer was laconic. "It'll keep Gulistan and Braley's bunch from reachin' their hideout through a hidden exit in the dead-end wall of the gorge. At the same time, it should start a little stampede that'll drive 'em backwards into the guns of Harry's crew."

Martin's tough, weathered features split in a hard grin. He nodded his appreciation, throughly sold on the idea.

Reed scouted along the plateau, locating boulders that were not too large and not too firmly entrenched to resist being shoved into space. He found two slabs close together and perched precariously close to the rim.

"We'll start here," he said and waited.

Twenty minutes went by and the thunder of hoofs became louder.

"Here they come!" Martin finally announced.

All three men stood briefly to watch a dark

307

moving tide of beef rumble forward through the defile. Here and there along the flanks of the herd, mounted riders urged the steers along with shouts and swinging rope ends.

20

NEARER and nearer that heaving sea of bodies came. Reed went to one of the boulders. Martin and the other puncher joined him. They leaned their weight against a rock, straining every muscle, booted feet sliding in the rubble.

The rock teetered on the edge, then slowly slid forward to pitch down the precipitous, slanting slope. In tremendous bounces it cascaded toward the bottom of the gorge. In its wake came hundreds of smaller stones, loosened by its passage.

Atop the mesa the three men toiled on with a feverish desperation to send several more boulders plunging into space. A thunderous roar filled the canyon as the booming landslide piled up a small mountain of debris in the dizzy depths below.

A thick curtain of dust billowed toward the sky. Cattle began bawling in panic. Horsemen down in the defile screamed in rage and fear. Guns bellowed. Looking through the pall of dust, Reed saw the leaders of the herd mill and tangle.

The cattle were hopelessly bunched. Horns clacked against horns. Steers were trampled to get free of those crushing tons of rock plummeting down the shaly slopes. Two riders went down, vanishing beneath a sea of pounding hoofs.

Two or three bullets ricocheted off the rocks on the mesa rim. But the sounds were lost in the clamor that tore the night apart. Only the spraying of rock chips in Reed's face warned him that he and his helpers had been discovered.

"Let's go!" he directed. "We've got a tough ride back the way we came."

He turned and raced to the spot where Sally was holding the horses. They mounted in a hurry and lashed the horses into a dead run across the plateau.

"If we don't outrun those buskies down there we may be trapped ourselves on that ledge trail," Dell Martin pointed out gloomily.

Reed gave him a stiff, straight glance. His eyes were hard and implacable, utterly without fear. Only when his gaze rested upon Sally did a tinge of regret color his cheeks.

"It's the risk we have to take," he murmured. "But I figure they'll be kept plenty busy avoidin' those panicky steers and lightin' a shuck outa the canyon to give much attention to the ledge trail." He turned to Sally. "I'm sorry you're in this."

"Don't be," she replied and quirted her horse to come abreast of the roan.

They hit the treacherous trail some minutes later. Already the moon had started its downward journey through the black, starlit vault of sky. Much of the canyon was in shadow. But Reed plunged the roan recklessly onto that narrow ribbon of beaten rock.

Far below them loomed the milling tangle of horses, cattle and men. Some of the beef had turned in a wider section of the canyon and were stampeding toward the exit. One or two riders, pinched in that wave of bodies, were thrown from their horses. Their brief cries of terror knifed into the night air, then were stilled as the stampede rolled over them.

Several hundred head of steers vanished through the canyon. Hundreds of others remained, charging back and forth in horrible confusion, trampling each other, locking horns and filling the night with their frantic bawling.

And all the while Reed, Sally and the other two men threaded their way down the slope. Three-quarters of the way to the bottom a small group of outlaws spotted them and opened fire.

Bullets whined through the air, but fell short. Reed kept on, holding his fire. Some of the outlaws sped through the canyon exit only to be met by a volley of lead from Wright's riders hidden beneath brush and rocks.

"It's workin'!" yelled Reed. He twisted once in the saddle, motioned Sally back. "Stay out of this."

Then he was plunging down the last few yards of the trail with Martin and the other man close behind him. Thundering Colts lashed their yellow-red streamers across the gloom. More outlaws swept through the gorge, racing out of the trap.

There were half a dozen of them and they whirled their mounts to face the menace of the trio of riders galloping toward them.

Reed's gun canted upward in his fist. He felt it buck solidly against his wrist, saw the red froth crawl from the bore. Then a leering outlaw lifted high in the stirrups and plunged to the ground.

Martin emptied a saddle before a bullet

drilled his left arm. He swore but fired again, dropping a horse. The renegade leaped clear, rolling over and over only to be pinned to earth by a slug from Reed's spouting forty-five.

Several wild-eyed steers lunged into view. Reed swerved out of their path. But two of the outlaws weren't quick enough. Sharp horns pierced their horses' flanks. The horses squealed in agony, sagged to their knees, throwing their riders beneath flashing steer hoofs.

Reed heard a yell behind him, saw three more riders bearing down upon him. Martin rushed in, firing as he came. One bulky man broke away from the rest, angling toward Reed's roan.

"We meet again, tin-star!" came the wild, reckless cry.

Reed recognized the voice of Jack Braley, the smiling but ruthless renegade leader.

"I reckon we've got you to thank for that landslide," Braley added, punctuating his words with a gushing stream of lead.

Reed felt the roan lurch and stagger as a bullet tunneled its chest. He freed his boots from the stirrups, jumped clear even as the roan pitched to its knees. A bullet raked the side of Reed's face as he landed in the rubble and rolled. Another slug chewed up dirt in front of him as Braley spurred toward him. The outlaw was a dark and menacing shape above Reed. Red death was crawling from Braley's gun.

Then Reed was on one elbow, flipping the hammer on two fast, well-centered shots. A change came over Braley's face. A spreading blotch of crimson dissolved his features. He slumped weakly over the horn. His horse ran on past Reed and crashed against the wall.

Yonder, near the canyon exit, there was a renewed burst of firing. At least fifteen of Gulistan's and Braley's crew were massing for an assault on Wright's positions. The riders bunched, went thundering forward at a signal from one of their group.

A deadly wave of gunfire swept from their weapons and was returned in feeble proportions by Wright's men. Two of the latter rose from their places of concealment, staggered out into the trail and fell down.

Then into that din of sound came the rumble of more hoofs. Reed's swift glance showed him a large body of horsemen approaching the defile. He made a rough guess that it was Sheriff Collier and one of the posses. They came on at a rapid run. Harry Wright was shouting at them as the outlaws bolted through his thin line of defense.

But now the odds had been evened and the renegades found themselves facing a double line of fire. Men locked together at close quarters firing their guns until they were empty, then clawing at each other with fists or knives.

Reed ran forward, clutched the dragging reins of a riderless horse and vaulted into the saddle. Automatically he shoved fresh cartridges into the firing chambers of his smoking Colt. He started toward the canyon exit but stopped when he heard a faint cry in the direction of the ledge trail. He saw a bulky rider storm across the gorge. Another slender figure rose up from a sheltering boulder. Reed's heart contracted. That slender figure was Sally. He saw her fire at the approaching rider. The shot was wild. Then she was falling down as the rider's gun roared and the galloping horse carried the man past her up the slope.

Rage vibrated through Reed's body in tremulous waves. He wheeled his mount, raked the heaving flanks with his spurs and charged after the bulky rider. Something about the man's big, wide shape in the saddle told Reed that it was Brad Gulistan.

Reed's heart was like a stone in his breast. He was recalling how Sally had fallen under the fire of Gulistan's red-flaming Colt, and a destructive urge lashed Reed on in headlong pursuit.

Two hundred yards up the twisting path Gulistan became aware of pursuit. He turned in the saddle. Ruby lights winked from his gun muzzle. Riding low over his mount's withers, Reed heard the slugs drone over his head.

He made no attempt to fire. Through narrowed, ferocious eyes he saw the distance between them lessen. He was utterly heedless of the treacherous nature of the trail.

Gulistan whirled about once more and fired. Reed felt the horse tremble beneath him and knew he was hit. But the animal kept on.

"You can't run away from my gun, Gulistan!" Reed roared.

In desperation Gulistan hauled in on the reins. The animal he was riding spooked up and reared high, forehoofs pawing the air. Sudden fear crawled into the rancher's face. His gun came up, centered on Reed.

"That's it, Gulistan! Take it in the chest!" Reed called and chopped down twice with his forty-five.

Both of his shots shaded Gulistan's. He saw Gulistan's wide-shouldered frame shake and twitch as if some giant hand were buffeting him. Then his horse lost its footing on the shaly, soft shoulder of the trail and carried him off into space.

Reed pulled his own horse in close to the canyon wall, and swung about carefully. He felt a curious let-down now that Gulistan was gone and the smell of burned gunpowder and thick dust was a raw, unpleasant smell in his nostrils.

Behind him the rattle of guns rose to a shrill crescendo, then slowly wavered and died. Immediately, then, men began yelling. In that turbulent shouting Reed detected a fierce note of triumph.

It sent him down the slope in a swift canter. Mounted men and others on foot milled about near the canyon exit. Reed's glance lingered upon the scene for only a brief moment. Then his eyes sought the cluster of rocks where he had last seen Sally.

His imagination was rebuilding the dread picture of her falling beneath the flame-lash of Gulistan's gun. It was a feverish torment in his blood and he was afraid that each stride of the

317

horse would bring him upon her bullet-crushed body.

He was still twenty yards from the boulders when Sally drifted out of the deep shadow of an overhang. She ran toward him and there was no sign of faltering or of weakness in her steps.

Skidding his mount to a halt, Reed swung to the ground. They met by the horse's head. Reed's hands went out to her firm, rounded shoulders and gripped them with an intense pressure that put a twinge of pain upon her lips.

"Sally, you don't know how glad I am to see that you're not hurt." The words came from Reed in a wild rush. His eyes clung to her smoothly molded features as if no power could ever make them look away. "When Gulistan fired at you I thought he'd—killed you."

"No, Jim," she whispered and her slender fingers fumbled nervously with the frayed edge of his calfskin vest. "I threw myself down and the bullet passed over me." The faint smile vanished from her lips. "You—got Gulistan?"

"Yeah. He's somewhere down-canyon where his horse carried him off the ledge trail when my bullets struck him."

A rising clamor in the gorge pulled them around. Reed's hands dropped away from

Sally's shoulders. The fight was over. The sprawled forms of wounded and dead men described a horrible pattern on the ground.

Occasionally a few wild-eyed steers bounded out of the canyon, striking out for the sandy plain beyond the V-notch of the defile. And moving toward Reed and Sally was a bunch of men, herding in front of them the remnants of the outlaws who had surrendered.

Harry Wright, nursing a bloody broken arm, led the group. Behind him, also wounded but looking savagely satisfied, came Clark Esmond and Val Ormand. Sheriff Collier was busy lining up his prisoners against the canyon wall, putting them under heavy guard, and supervising first-aid measures for some of the wounded cowpunchers and possemen.

"What happened to Braley and Gulistan?" Harry Wright asked Reed bluntly.

"Both dead," said Reed and explained briefly.

"Reed, you're a hard man to beat," broke in Clark Esmond. There was a scarlet furrow on his gaunt cheek and a dark stain high up on his shirt. "You've put everyone in Outpost in your debt. Wright gave us most of the story a few minutes ago. If we'd known you were a US

319

marshal you might have made things easier for yourself."

Reed shrugged, his smile thin and remote.

"It doesn't always work out that way," he said. "My experience has been that I accomplish more in a strange town by keeping my identity under cover. You will remember the attempt on my life by Luke Stacey, who was a Wright puncher secretly employed by Gulistan. Stacey tried to kill me because Gulistan knew I was a marshal and wanted me out of the way.

"The main point is that Gulistan and Braley have been smashed. From now on there'll be no more rustling in Outpost. It'll be a fairly simple matter to round up the beef in the morning and cut out your own brands as well as those of your neighbors.

"I never did get a chance to query Gulistan about the money stolen from the bank. But I reckon you'll find it cached either at Gulistan's place or in Braley's hideout on the other side of this blind canyon."

"Accordin' to one of Gulistan's hands who talked after he took a little lead into his system, the money is at the Circle G," said Val Ormand.

Clark Esmond, tall and thin and suddenly ill

at ease, was glancing at Sally. He cleared his throat nervously before speaking.

"Sally," he said with a deep and sincere regret showing in his gaunt face, "it's rather late to be making apologies, but if anyone ever got a raw deal from a town it was you and your brother. I hold myself to blame for that as well as others here in Outpost." He looked at Ormand and Wright. "That includes both of you."

"I admit it," replied Wright. "None of us ever gave Johnny a chance because of your father. Maybe if I'd hired him when he asked for a job on the Slash W he might never have turned wild and gotten into a tight spot with Gulistan. I'd like to make it up to you somehow—"

"There is one way," said Clark Esmond quickly. "And that's to offer you your job as school teacher again—and to say that as long as I'm in Outpost you'll never need to worry about anything."

Sally ran a slender hand through her curly hair. Her tanned face was streaked with dirt. Somehow it lent an odd strength and beauty to her features. But in her eyes there still lingered the dull sheen of bitterness and grief.

321

"Thanks," she murmured, "but I've decided to leave Outpost."

"Why?" demanded Wright.

"There's nothing to hold me here."

She turned away from them then. For just an instant her eyes lifted to Reed's mute and expectant. He watched her soberly, his features becoming heavy under the somber wash of his thoughts.

Reed was not aware of the gravity of his expression. Therefore, he was puzzled when he saw the light of expectancy die in Sally's eyes and she walked on past him.

Some strange urgency over which he had no control sent him after her. They left Wright and Esmond and the others in an awkward, whispering group. Reed's hand was hard upon Sally's arm. Its pressure pulled her around to face him.

"Where will you go?" he asked, a little annoyed with himself because his voice sounded thick and odd.

She smiled faintly, almost mockingly. There was a mixture of hope and despair in the tanned contour of her cheeks.

"Any place but Outpost," she replied.

Reed's mind was full of this girl. Her nearness was an imperative call to his senses. Always before this he had considered his own bleak and dangerous existence to be complete.

But since she had nursed him back to life at her cabin this long-held personal conviction no longer carried weight. He knew as surely as he had ever known anything that this girl with a spirit as strong as his own and with the wildness of this land in her blood, filled an urgent need within himself.

"Wait, Sally," he said with an odd dryness in his throat. "There's someone in Outpost who cares a heap about where you go."

Her eyes widened warmly upon him.

"Who is that?" she asked in a taut whisper.

"Fellow by the name of Reed," he replied with a wry grin. His hands reached out for her and gripped her upper arms, holding her body rigid, forcing her eyes up to meet his. "I've got a feeling inside of me that if I left here knowing it would be the last time to see you, I'd never know any peace or contentment.

"I've watched you brace yourself against a whole town, seeing in your battle, a battle I've had over and over. I've an idea that whatever we might face from now on would be handled that much better if we faced it together.

"There isn't much a federal lawman can offer a woman. It's a hard life and a lonely one— dingy hotel rooms in hostile towns and always the endless manhunt and the thought that never leaves you: that this may be your last job. It'll mean long weeks of waiting, wondering if I'm ever coming back—"

Reed's arms relaxed their pressure. Sally slid inside his arms, came against him. She tilted her face and her eyes were brighter than he could ever remember them.

"Do you think I'd mind the waiting, Jim? Do you think I'd mind the loneliness or the emptiness while you're away so long as I knew you'd be coming back to *me*?"

Jim Reed bent his head and his lips came down upon Sally's mouth and lingered there while the loneliness slowly left him and the thought came to him that from this moment on life would have real meaning.

TOP HAND
by Wade Everett

The Broken T was big enough for a man on the run to hire out as a cowhand and be safe. But no ranch is big enough to let a man hide from himself.

GUN WOLVES OF LOBO BASIN
by Lee Floren

The Feud was a blood debt. When Smoke Talbot found the outlaws who gunned down his folks he aimed to nail their hide to the barn door.

SHOTGUN SHARKEY
by Marshall Grover

The westbound coach carrying the indomitable Larry and Stretch and their mixed bag of allies headed for a shooting showdown.

RIFLES ON THE RANGE
by Lee Floren

Doc Mike and the farmer stood there alone between Smith and Watson. Doc Mike knew what was coming. There was this moment of stillness, a clock-tick of eternity, and then the roar would start. And somebody would die . . .

HARTIGAN
by Marshall Grover

Hartigan had come to Cornerstone to die. He chose the time and the place, but he did not fight alone. Side by side with Nevada Jim, the territory's unofficial protector, they challenged the killers—and Main Street became a battlefield.

HARSH RECKONING
by Phil Ketchum

The minute Brand showed up at his ranch after being illegally jailed, people started shooting at him. But five years of keeping himself alive in a brutal prison had made him tough and careless about who he gunned down . . .

FIGHTING RAMROD
by Charles N. Heckelmann

Most men would have cut their losses, but Frazer counted the bullets in his guns and said he'd soak the range in blood before he'd give up another inch of what was his.

LONE GUN
by Eric Allen

Smoke Blackbird had been away too long. The Lequires had seized the Blackbird farm, forcing the Indians and settlers off, and no one seemed willing to fight! He had to fight alone.

THE THIRD RIDER
by Barry Cord

Mel Rawlins wasn't going to let anything stand in his way. His father was murdered, his two brothers gone. Now Mel rode for vengeance.

RIDE A LONE TRAIL
by Gordon D. Shirreffs

The valley was about to explode into open range war. All it needed was the fuse and Ken Macklin was it.

ARIZONA DRIFTERS
by W. C. Tuttle
When drifting Dutton and Lonnie Steelman decide to become partners they find that they have a common enemy in the formidable Thurston brothers.

TOMBSTONE
by Matt Braun
Wells Fargo paid Luke Starbuck to outgun the silver-thieving stagecoach gang at Tombstone. Before long Luke can see the only thing bearing fruit in this eldorado will be the gallows tree.

HIGH BORDER RIDERS
by Lee Floren
Buckshot McKee and Tortilla Joe cut the trail of a border tough who was running Mexican beef into Texas. They stopped the smuggler in his tracks.

HARD MAN WITH A GUN
by Charles N. Heckelmann
After Bob Keegan lost the girl he loved and the ranch he had sweated blood to build, he had nothing left but his guts and his guns but he figured that was enough.